I0822432

RUIN ME

AN IMMORTAL VICES AND VIRTUES NOVEL

JENNA WOLFHART

Cover Art by Yocla Designs

Photography by Gene Mollica

NO MAN'S LAND

Several thousand years ago, a portal opened on Earth, bringing the first magical creatures into the world. Over time, more portals opened.

Houses were created. Supernaturals joined and formed a truce.

But there are those out there who are not so lucky. Those stuck in a lawless city, ruled by vampire gangs. With no House to back them up, they have to fend for themselves.

Welcome to No Man's Land.

CHAPTER I
SILAS

It's strange living in a city full of monsters. You start to think you're one of them, all darkness, deceit, and revenge, especially in my case. Instead of giving me a Lego set on my eighth birthday, my vampire mother extracted me from our lavishly decorated townhouse and deposited me in the city slums, just to get me out of her hair for awhile. Within those contorted alleys, I plotted the hostile takedown of her empire. Needless to say, the rebellion never happened.

Now, twenty years later, I'm out of the slums but still on the streets. I prowl through the concrete maze with the buildings' red bricks emanating a foul odor of rot and blood. And the evil creeps up on me, like a slithering snake winding its way up my leg and into my heart.

It's a dark and quiet night in Towton City, a haven for Houseless supernaturals about two hours west of New York, smack dab in lawless No Man's Land. Here, we're not under the jurisdiction of any of the eight Houses scattered across the globe, formed after a portal opened in Portland that exposed all the supernaturals that live in this world. It means freedom, in a way. But it also means total chaos. I've contacted Earth and Emerald a few times over the years for help, but they've got their hands full. Besides, they don't like people who cause issues, and this whole city is one big problem. And half of our residents are humans.

A thick cloud of smoke puffs into the January sky from the power station stacks—they're still running, somehow—and obscures the moon from view. I lurk in the shadowed doorframe of an abandoned storefront and watch the Downtown windows blink out one by one until there is nothing left, until there is only me. Me and a plethora of other vampires, shifters, and fae, but there will be one fewer in number after tonight. It won't do the city any good; the streets are far too steeped in grime to ever get clean. I do it because someone has to scrub at the black spots, no matter how permanent they are.

Hooking my fists under the body's armpits, I drag it into the middle of the silent street. I caught this guy stalking a shifter girl home from her waitressing job at Four Points Pizzeria, his knife glinting in the moonlight. He likely wanted her blood. I shot him in the head with a vampire bullet, and that was that. He'll never hurt that girl now. Or anyone else.

His vacant eyes stare up at me. According to his ID, he's Nicky Tanner, a member of one of the vampire gangs. A trickle of blood runs down his face and pools onto the pavement. It's not often enough I take out one of these guys, and this one will send the appropriate message.

"I'm watching you," I say into the night. "Enjoy cleaning up the mess."

I trace my steps toward the slums and flick up the brim of my black baseball cap, my eyes spotlighting every detail of my surroundings. An abandoned sneaker, skittering on a wave of cigarette butts. An open window on the second floor of the building on my right, no curtains, no blinds. A yellowed flyer advertising a missing sister, lightly flapping against a utility pole in the frosty breeze. Street lamps loom overhead, but few emit any light. Most of the lightbulbs have been smashed. I sidestep the jagged shards to avoid making any noise. The second you let down your guard in this place, the second you're less like a person—or vampire, in my case—and more like a corpse.

A *crunch*. I freeze, feet in mid-step. Even though I normally blend into the darkness, something doesn't feel right. Eyes are on me. Usually my enemies don't know I'm near until it's too late for them to do a damn thing about it.

Slipping my hand into my pocket to finger my gun, I eye the street before me. Nothing there other than an emptiness swallowing up the space where cars and buses rumble by during daylight hours. Slowly, I turn. Nothing there either. Someone else skulks along these streets, and anyone hugging the darkness is surely someone on my long list of supernaturals to hunt.

And he just saw me dump the body.

In a flicker, a hulking form materializes. Tall and full of shadows. Oh, it's *him*. Phantom.

I take a step back as he grabs for my arm. He narrows his eyes, half-hidden behind a dark mask. In his black full-body kevlar, he looms like some kind of wicked sentry of the night, but I'm not the slightest bit intimidated. I'm bigger than he is. And much more deadly. Still, I lower the brim of my hat and stand a bit taller.

"Orpheus." He addresses me using my alter-ego name, in a voice so low it rumbles deep in his chest.

"Why are you Downtown?" I ask. "You never come here. I thought you didn't like the smell."

He shifts closer, and the broken glass crunches under his leather boots. "That was as much your decision as it was mine."

That's true. Two years ago, I approached Phantom about splitting the city patrol in half, each of us taking on a territory each. In the absence of a House, we decided to do something about this place ourselves. I took Downtown with the Nightshade vampire gang and the Coils. I suggested he take Uptown with Blackthorn, as much a dig at him than anything else. Blackthorn is the city's other vampire gang, but they've been quiet the past few years after Phantom drove their leader out of the city. The leader who just so happens to be my mother.

He should have destroyed her. But he won't. He's a terrible hunter with too many rules. He never kills, even if it means a murderer runs free to torment the lives of more innocents.

"You didn't answer my question." I twist my mouth into something resembling a smile, but I haven't smiled a real smile in years. If ever.

Phantom curls his hands into tight fists, his leather gloves crackling like gunshots. "I need to talk to you."

"So, go on then." He's trying to set me on edge, but I don't intend to let him bully me around. Leaning back on my heels, I unbutton my coat. The material billows in the smoggy breeze, revealing what I have hidden underneath. Phantom's eyes flick down to the sheathed knife on my belt. Two can play at this game.

He widens his stance and crosses his arms over his chest. "Give me this block tonight. I've got something to take care of."

"Again?" I frown. This is the third time in the past month Phantom has asked me to walk away from this particular block for a night. The first time I thought nothing of it. The second time, I had some mild suspicion. But this third time is bringing on full-blown warning bells, clanging against my skull. Phantom is up to something, and I need to know what it is. "There's nothing happening here. I'm only passing through to keep an eye on the streets near the slums."

Instead of answering verbally, he nods. He has an irritating habit of doing that.

"I'll agree to it," I say after a long pause. "But only if you tell me what you're doing. If this is about the Coils, I need to know. Those humans can't protect themselves."

"Nothing to do with that." He answers so quickly that it's obvious there's no point in arguing. What could he possibly be hiding? Phantom has always been forthright with me about his extracurricular activities, especially when it involves someone who's really crossed a line.

A little worm wiggles inside my brain, and it asks if the unimaginable has happened, if Phantom has turned. My blood runs cold. If he ever supported one of the gangs, Phantom would be an abominable force. He's strong, powerful, and because of his day job, he has access to so many assets. I need to snuff this out before it can truly begin. Find out if corruption swirls through his veins, and if so, then expose and dispose.

"Nevermind." I shrug my hands into my pockets. "I'll go home. I'm not opposed to a night off. Just make sure this street stays clean." If he won't tell me what he's up to, then I'll just have to find out for myself whether he's been consumed by the darkness.

"Don't worry. I know the drill." He scans the block. "I patrolled these streets for a couple years…"

Before you came along, is the unspoken ending to that sentence.

Even though Phantom didn't give much of an argument against the city patrol split, he's never seemed thrilled by my involvement. Because while he gave forth his story, I did not give forth mine. It's a piece of information he will never know. I think it unnerves him, coping with the fact that I know he is Damian

Kane, a century old angel and the owner of half the city's real estate, while his guesses at my identity have been wildly off-base.

That and the fact I kill.

"Enjoy your evening."

I turn my back and stroll away, melting into the shadows. When I've gone no more than half a block, I step into a darkened doorframe to watch the black-clad vigilante's next move. He's still standing motionless underneath the broken street lamp, staring into the shadows where I've disappeared and no doubt waiting to ensure I've left him alone on the street.

One thing about Phantom. He's a good tracker. I wouldn't go so far as to say he's extraordinary, but he's pretty damn good. Three years ago, he managed to tail my mother. After several hours, she led him straight to the Downtown docks where she slaughtered a group of humans trying to escape. He ran her out of Towton after that, and I have to admit, the city has been better off ever since. At least in Uptown.

But as good as Phantom is at tracking, I'm better. Whatever he's doing tonight, I'll witness every moment, because I can stick to him like blood to a vampire's fangs. And if he's joined any of the rogue supernatural gangs, I'll have no choice but to take out the closest thing to a savior this city has ever seen.

It's a good thing I brought my gun out tonight.

CHAPTER 2
GWEN

It's almost two o'clock in the morning, and I still haven't gotten to punch something. A steady drizzle started fifteen minutes ago, splashing into my eyeballs and smearing my hand-painted domino mask so that black blobs of kohl now run down my cheeks. I sigh when the power station clock tower bangs out the chime for the hour. Where the hell is he?

I pull the hood of my sweatshirt tighter around the top of my frizzing dark hair and glare out at the empty street from my hiding place behind a dumpster. This is seriously not sane. My teeth begin to chatter, jaws drumming out a beat more like Adele than the Rocky theme. But if I leave my post, someone's going to get a beat down, and that someone will definitely be me.

But whatever. Fuck this. I'm so over waiting.

I clomp out from behind the dumpster, wrinkling my nose at the sour odor that follows. Before I've even made it two steps, the whoosh of a fist is my only warning. I hop back just in time, boots kicking up rain water. The fist barely misses my face, so close that the knuckles skim one of the kohl blobs and knock it off my cheek. Black splats on the ground, joining the gazillion other stains that paint the pavement.

That was close.

Quick scan of my attacker: over six feet, clad in an all-black suit made out of some thick armor-type material, with a mask covering his face but not his flashing eyes. I swing my leg and kick my foot up at his jaw, one of the few areas not shielded by the kevlar. He grabs my ankle in a chokehold, ripping my black leggings and scratching my skin with his gloves. Great. Another paired ruined.

Gritting my teeth, I yank my leg, but it only throws me off-balance, and my arms become windmills to keep me standing. He lets go, and I clatter onto the grimy pavement. My knees slam into the rough surface; my breath launches out of me. Ouch.

I look up, hood sliding off my hair. The dark, looming figure crosses his arms and stares down at me.

"Failed again."

"I was distracted by my destroyed clothes. Again. Thanks, Dad." I roll over and rub the spot where his grip on my ankle almost cut off my circulation. The leggings are toast, and I swear a hand-shaped bruise is already popping up on my ankle.

He glances around the empty street, the empty sidewalk. There's exactly zero other people out here tonight, but that doesn't stop his overblown paranoia. "Don't call me that. Not out in the streets. And put your hood up."

"Fine. That move was annoying, *Phantom*." I pull my hood back up, obscuring my face. The kohl lining my eyes like a mask usually helps hide my features, but right now I probably look more like a drowned mime than a badass vigilante-in-training.

"Stop kicking at my face. And I'll stop doing it." He shakes his head, and the lines around his mouth deepen. One of the signs he's frustrated with me. "You do it every time. You count on a signature move—"

"And then your enemies will figure it out and know you're coming." I push myself up from the concrete, internally groaning from my recent surplus of bruises, and dust off my leggings. It's no use, though. I'm an absolute mess. "I know, I know. Stop with the lecture."

He frowns. "You want me to train you or not?"

The truth is, I want nothing else. A lot of the people in this city want peace. Or escape. Me, I dream of taking my fist to a vampire's face. It's a pretty simple dream when you really think about it, but right now, Towton City is ruled by the gangs, and I can't just sit on my ass watching old sitcoms when I know I could be making a difference.

The humans stuck inside the Coils need my help.

Instead of saying all this, I ask, "Can this training be of the variety that doesn't involve me transforming into an ice sculpture behind a dumpster?"

"Stop complaining. You need to know how to fight on the ground, since your wings rarely work. And you also need to learn how to do more than throw a good left hook."

Grinning, I blow on my numb fingers, but it's his unintentional compliment that gives me a flicker of warmth. "Ha. You said it. So you do think I have a good left hook."

"Don't make me take it back. Cockiness can get you killed." He crosses his kevlar-covered arms over his chest, which somehow makes him look bigger. At normal times, Dad's six foot frame towers over me, even though I'm pushing five seven. But when he's doing his Phantom thing, like right now, I'm an ant in front of him. "You were loud again."

I sigh and glance behind me at the dumpster I'd chosen as my lookout point. I was sure I'd hidden myself from view this time, but apparently not. He knew exactly where I was while I totally failed at spotting him. Of course, there's a reason they call him Phantom. He didn't come up with the name himself. No one else moves the way he does, as if he's vapor, smoke, mist. Not even vampires can be that stealthy. His feet don't slap the ground, and his clothes don't crinkle when he walks. Sometimes I wonder if he even bothers to breathe.

And while that's great for him, it's never really been my approach to the whole thing. Run in and kick some ass, that's my motto. But my motto is what's kept me doing this same stupid exercise over and over again. I'm not powerful as far as angels are concerned, so I have to rely on my fighting skills.

"How'd you know I was there?" I pull the hood further down over my forehead and imagine myself as invisible, but I never will be to him.

"You're loud and reckless. Gotta work on your stealth."

A scream rips through the quiet pitter-patter of rain. A woman's scream, high-pitched and frantic. When it stops, a heavy blanket of silence falls in its place. My breath catches, and I whirl around. The only thing that moves is a missing person's flyer, ripped from its pole in a sudden gust.

"I thought you said this block was abandoned." Curling my hands into fists, I bend my legs into fight-stance mode. There's a reason my father picked this block for training. To get me out from behind four walls and a roof without letting me actually do anything. No one's lived on this block for years, so there's no one here for the vampire gang to harass.

That scream sure as hell was real, though.

"Go to your apartment." My father's voice holds so much authority that I can't help but glance up at him. His lips are set in a hard line. His back is straight, arms hung loosely at his side.

Completely unfazed by the fact we just heard a blood-curdling scream at two o'clock in the morning.

"We should help her," I say.

"Gwen." My father places a heavy hand on my shoulder and squeezes. I grip my fists tighter. He must have spotted something, though as far as I can tell, there's nothing here but us, just two crazies literally chilling out in a January downpour, heads cocked and listening for the next scream.

Wait a second. There's no way I heard that right. My father said my name. In the streets. That is not a good sign.

"I don't see anything," I say in a rush. Though something is definitely off. A smell drifts toward us: the hint of cigarettes and, frankly, a bit of B.O.

Before my dad can respond, blurry shadows morph into moving bodies. Several large men whisper out from the darkness, faces covered by ski masks. I stiffen. My eyes immediately flick to their biceps to spot the vampire loyalty tattoo that must be there, but their arms are completely hidden by slick rain jackets. Still, they must be in one of the gangs. Likely Nightshade. Blackthorn vampires don't tend to venture Downtown.

Quick scan of attackers: five of them, which is coincidentally the exact number of a Nightshade crew, all at least twice my size and clearly hiding who they are with the ski mask thing, which I prefer to view as a plus. It means they might not want to kill us. Maybe.

As vicious as the vampires are, they know better than to go after angels.

"Run," Dad says to me.

Even though my mind screams to listen to him, I hold my ground.

"Not so fast," one of the vampires says, and then turns to the others. "Don't let her get away."

The one on the end edges closer to me. The bottom of his jeans drags behind him, drenched from the puddles seizing control of the streets. I narrow my eyes and try to detect anything at all that could reveal his identity, but the ski mask and the rain jacket make that impossible.

As part of my training, my father tests me on names, faces, and titles of every known member and associate of the vampire gangs, along with their place within their network. I've got most of them memorized. Things seem to change a lot from week to week, but I'd still know a face if I saw one.

"If you let her go now," my father says, "no one will get hurt."

A couple of the vampires laugh, and that's all it takes to propel my father into action.

His right leg swooshes up and slams into the closest vamp's face. *Crunch*. Droplets of blood arc through the air.

Wet jeans guy moves in to block me from joining. I grunt and jab my left hook into his stomach. He barely flinches, but I'm not done yet. Bending my knees, I throw all my power into my fist and smash an uppercut into his jaw. He stumbles back and swipes away a trail of blood leaking out of his lip.

A blur in the corner of my eye. There's another one. This vamp reaches out to grab me, but I swoop down to dodge his greedy hands. I smile. It's obvious they're only trying to stop me, not hurt me. Their mistake. My palms flat on the wet pavement, I sweep out my leg, using all my angel strength to crash it into the back of his knees before he knows what's happening.

Bullseye. He falls flat on his ass. I can't help but grin as I pop back up into boxing stance and twirl to face the next attacker.

There's only a few facts I register.

Absolutely massive. Bright red eyes. Arms hurtling toward me. I dodge left. He tries again, but I sidestep just in time. Gritting my teeth, I throw myself into my left hook, and my fist slams into a slab of bricks. My hand crunches. Fire licks my knuckles. I bite the insides of my cheeks and drop back a few steps, shaking my hand.

Someone grabs me from behind. I twist to get free, but thick arms snake around my neck. They squeeze tight, cutting off the air I'm desperately gasping. I stomp my heel down to smash the vampire's toes, but he shifts his foot just in time.

"Nuh uh," he whispers in my ear as fangs scraped against my exposed throat. "Won't get away with that trick on me. I've got four sisters."

Come on, Gwen. I am so much better than this, but my training hasn't covered an overgrown vampire suffocating me with his biceps. I reach my hands behind me and claw at the vamp's face. My nails dig in, and he jerks his arm tighter around my neck. Lungs burning, I gasp for air and choke on the rain that flies into my throat. The vampire loosens his grip on me, but only barely. Sweet air sails into my lungs.

"Let her go." For the first time in forever, my father's voice sounds shaky. I want to see his face, but the vampire holding me squeezes out a warning when I try to twist my head. "What is it that you want?"

This obviously isn't some random confrontation. These vampires were prepared. A whole crew, hiding their identities so we couldn't point the finger later. Plus, no one punches, kicks, and otherwise maims a Nightshade member and gets to live. Unless they want something.

"The girl is obviously important to you, so we're going to make a deal." The leader of the crew steps forward. There's only a handful of people he might be. Our makeshift boxing ring here is just on the upper edge of the Southern Heights neighborhood, which is the territory of Albert Armone's crew, popularly known as the Mad Hatter. He's pretty infamous in Towton City, with his ever-changing hats to reflect his mood. Even though he's never been caught doing a single thing, he's known for wandering around the city playing handwritten songs about blood rage on his ukulele. Videos end up getting sent around. Everybody watches them. But the thing is, this guy sounds nothing like Albert Armone.

"What. Is it. That you want," my father says. If he could kill people with his voice, these vampires would be dead right about now.

"We want you to come with us into the Coils." Not-Armone smiles, stretching the ski mask around his flaking lips. "And we'll let the girl go, completely unharmed."

"No!" I pull against my captor. His arm tightens around me, and I dig my nails into his rain jacket, fingers sliding against the slippery material.

"That's it?"

"That's it." Not-Armone spreads his hands in front of him as if they're discussing a simple barter instead of my father's impending death.

He can't go into the Coils. He just can't.

"Done," my father says.

No, no, no. I squeeze my eyes tight, beads of sweat popping up on my forehead. My father can't go in there or he might never come out again. It's not that the slums—known in Towton City as The Coils—are inherently dangerous, even though a lot of bad stuff goes down in there. It's not that I'm totally naive about the fact he often frequents the place when he's in Phantom mode. It's that the Coils are where people like these guys dispose of their enemies. Through the twisting and turning alleys, in the impossible darkness, anything can happen in the slums without anyone ever knowing about it.

It's only half a block to the single Downtown entrance into

the Coils. When Dad turns and walks away from me, he's led by Not-Armone and two vamps who must be Soldiers. Their bodies slowly morph into blurry, gray blobs, and all I can do is struggle helplessly against my captor as they disappear into the rain-soaked night. After an unbearable ten minutes has passed, the vampire holding me finally lets me go.

I stumble forward, rushing after my father. Nobody tries to stop me. My boots pound through the rain, step after step, until I'm standing just across the street from the entrance. Looking up, I set my eyes upon the sight I've been avoiding all night. Ten floors loom above. Sagging, yellowed blocks of apartments, stacked one on top of the other. Windows are broken, dim fluorescent lighting slipping out through the jagged holes. Every single level, every single window, every single minuscule balcony is caged over with bars. To keep people out. And to keep the humans in.

It's exactly the same as it was the last time I saw the Coils in person. Twenty years ago. The day…it happened. Static pours into my head, a loud crackling that blocks out the rest of the world. In my mind's eye, my mother's face flashes. A face full of pain. Stomach turning, I throw a palm over my lips to gulp back the nausea threatening to heave my earlier tuna sandwich onto the sidewalk. I squeeze my eyes tight. *Don't think about it, Gwen. Don't think about it.*

The vision of her heart-shaped face fades from my mind, but the nausea doesn't budge an inch. Vomit burns the back of my throat. Air can't fill my lungs fast enough. Leaning over, I grab my knees and wipe my sweaty palms on my leggings. I can't breathe, I can't think, and my vision is turning black at the edges, tunneling smaller and smaller, until the only thing I can see is the entrance to the Coils.

CHAPTER 3
SILAS

Ruses come in many forms, and this one came in the form of a non-existent damsel in distress. I found an old boombox, turned up to maximum volume, playing the sound of a woman screaming. And now, Phantom has disappeared from where I last saw him. This doesn't fit well, like a size-too-small pair of boots, scraping bloody blisters onto your heels. I round the block and scan the street. Just across from the Coils, Gwen Kane is bowed over, her body shaking from erratic breaths.

Gwen Kane. Something strange stirs in my stomach. That's why he was here. I take in her dark clothes, the kohl around her eyes, understanding at once. He's training her. It makes sense. Gwen is full throttle in everything she does. When she marches down the street, people notice. It's the way she carries herself, head up, shoulders back. Eyes full of fire. You know if you cross her, you'll regret every moment of it. A lot like Phantom, though a much rawer, much more earnest version of him.

I know all this because…I've spent years noticing Gwen Kane.

She's my mate, not that she has any idea of it. And I've never told her, either. We're both better off without a mate bond complicating our lives.

Still, I want to reach out from the shadows and stop her shoulders from shaking. It's as if the mere sight of the Coils has her crumbling to her knees. *Where is Phantom?*

The low hum of an engine catches my attention. I twist my head to eye the end of the block, and the nose of a black car pokes around the corner. Flashing silver and gold lights strobe color onto the washed-out buildings. The Saints are here, a group of angels who formed their own gang when vampires started trying to target them for blood. Frowning, I glance back at Gwen.

They'd never hurt one of their own, but Gwen is half-human. They're just as likely to throw her into the Coils as they are to help her.

I dash toward her hunched figure. The closer I get, the more I feel as if an invisible rope is pulling me back. Maybe this is a terrible mistake. Stories of my Orpheus assassin persona has spread through the city like a virus. Even if her father has mentioned our arrangement to her, how will she react when she sees me? She'll know who I am.

When I reach her, I opt for clearing my throat rather than physical confrontation. She gasps and twists up to face me. Her deep brown eyes widen, her face streaked with black. Drenched clothes sagging on her curvy frame, there's a strange hollowed out look about her. Somehow, I can't help but think, this doesn't stop her from looking…fucking amazing. Cheeks flushed and eyes wild, there's just so much life bursting from her. She takes a step away from me but thrusts her shoulders back and fists her hands as if she's not sure whether she's choosing fight or flight.

I hold my hands up as a show of peace. "The Saints are coming. You should get out of here."

She squints. "I know that coat. You're Orpheus."

The lights flash a silver and gold projection onto Gwen's face. We need to move, now. I touch her arm. For a moment, the world pauses. She doesn't jerk away, and her eyes meet mine, and it's as if she suddenly sees. Suddenly understands what I've known for years. *We're mates*. I find myself holding my breath. A beat passes. And another. Before a siren wails to life, jolting me back into reality.

Pulling on Gwen's arm, I drag her to the closest abandoned storefront. The door hangs crooked on its rotting frame. I kick it open and duck inside. Gwen rips her arm away and hesitates before shaking her head and stepping in behind me. Dust swirls as I throw the door shut.

I step over jutted up floorboards forming a warped plywood mountain between me and the windows coated with a thick layer of dust. Swiping away a circle of grime, I peer outside. Gwen joins me without saying a word and scribbles out her own circle on the window with the sleeve of her hoodie. I watch her out of the corner of my eye. Her face is ashen, but her eyes are unblinking, unyielding. Whatever was breaking her outside has cracked away and left behind a raw, beautiful sort of strength that can only be seen in those who have been to hell and survived.

Three cars swerve to a stop outside the Coils. A figure silhouetted by their headlights stands in the middle of the street, and the angels spill from their cars with gleaming swords raised.

"Stop!" The angel's voice booms.

Gwen gasps and presses her face against the glass. The figure takes two steps forward, easing into the swirling lights. Tall and full of shadows. It's Phantom, with a pistol in one hand and an abstract painting of blood on the other. The mystery of Phantom's disappearance is solved, but something still doesn't fit. I glance at Gwen, expecting a kaleidoscope of emotion to form a disconsolate pattern on her face, but instead, she almost smiles.

"Drop the gun, Phantom," one of the angels calls out.

Phantom drops the pistol, and it clatters onto the pavement, followed by a waterfall of cartridges. Even muffled through the windows, the *clink* against the ground is unmistakable. Why would he have a handful of bullets? The short answer is he wouldn't. The longer answer is an even bigger question than that.

"Turn around," the angel says. "Put your hands on your head. We're taking you to the cathedral, Phantom."

Phantom obeys, silent while the Saints tighten rope around his wrists. This is definitely a first. For years, the Saints have looked the other way when it comes to Phantom's nighttime excursions. Even though he refuses to join their gang, they don't really care what he does as long as he doesn't target angels.

"What exactly happened?" I ask Gwen.

She stiffens at the sound of my voice, and a long pause stretches out the seconds ticking by. "We got ambushed by five vampires. Nightshade, I think. They took Phantom into the Coils. I tried to do something, but..."

"Who were they? Did you recognize them?"

"No. Their faces were covered." She shifts away from me as if she's trying to give me an unspoken signal that she's done talking. These vampires must have known I was skulking around tonight. So, they distracted me with the scream before attacking Phantom. Three of us at once would have been far too much for them to handle.

The Saints put Phantom into a car, and the sirens choke off mid-scream. Gwen shoves away from the window, leaving behind a vacuum of cold air.

"Where are you going?" I sidestep in front of her.

"Get out of my way."

So, that's how it's going to be, then. She's going to ignore what I know she felt—that we're mates. Fine with me.

"It's a bad idea. If they see you, they'll probably want to take you in, too, and you won't be given the same level of respect that they'll give him."

"I'm not an idiot." She crosses her arms and lifts her chin. "Phantom and I have a protocol for this kind of situation. Now, move."

A *protocol*. I almost smile. Clearly, I haven't given her enough credit. In fact, everything she's done tonight has given me this impression.

"We've never been properly introduced." I hold out a gloved hand. She flicks her eyes down, and back up again, but doesn't move an inch.

"Trust me, I know who you are."

"Of course. And you are?" I raise my eyebrows. I don't expect her to tell me her name is Gwen Kane, but surely she has something else she likes to go by when she's out hunting in the streets.

"Yeah, this isn't happening."

"What isn't?"

"This." She points a shaky finger at me, then at herself. "Friendship is a no go. I don't care if we're on the same side. You're a murderer."

"I see. You're welcome."

"What?"

"Here's some advice." Slowly, I begin buttoning my coat, whisking my knife and everything else exposed out of sight. "The next time someone helps you, don't insult him."

For few moments, the space between us is punctuated by

silence. Her insult hit me harder than I care to admit and definitely more than I care to show. Yes, I have killed people, but it's always been in retaliation against their depravity. With the ruthless, you have to be ruthless yourself. She doesn't understand that, and I knew she wouldn't. She is Phantom's daughter, after all. Holding out an olive branch of friendship was a ludicrous idea, even if she is my fated mate. *Especially* since she's my mate. We should stay far away from each other.

"I didn't need your help." She turns and walks toward the corridor that will lead her to the back alley.

I let out a sharp laugh. "Right. You had the situation entirely under control."

"What's that supposed to mean?" She freezes at the edge of the room.

"You were having a panic attack. While fighting a vampire gang. Sounds like a dangerous combination to me. You'd be delusional to think otherwise."

"Fuck off." She stomps into the darkness, and a moment later, a door slam reverberates throughout the entire building.

Good riddance. If Gwen Kane is going to hurl emotional punches at me, then I will hurl them right back. My blood buzzes from the encounter, and I stand for several moments in the stillness of the room to push the jarred pieces of my composure back into place. Of course she assumes the worst in me, even though all she knows is second-hand information.

It doesn't matter anyway, I tell myself. There are much more pressing things to focus on right now. Something fucked up has happened here tonight, and I intend to find out what it is.

After waiting several moments in the storefront's quiet dark for the Saints to drive away, I cross the street and stoop under the metal archway entrance of the slums, a jagged, maw-like thing that gives off the impression of an eager pair of jaws.

Inside, a twisting, turning worm of an alley stretches out before me. Overhead, the cables sparking with magic-based electricity are incalculable, and the sky can only be seen from several stories above. The air is thick and full of mold, and this corridor is so narrow that my elbows skim each side as I walk.

After a few yards, I stop at the first doorway on my left, a doorway with no door. Inside, a small, balding human man sits on a rickety chair, hunched over and petting a mewing cat in his lap. His figure is more diminished than it usually is and his skin more pockmarked than the last time I saw him. Along the metal walls, row upon row of knock-off amulets sit ready for sale. A dingy lightbulb hangs in the middle of the room as still as a statue. There's no breeze inside the Coils.

"Ronan," I say. "You're up late as always."

He stays just as he is, quietly petting his cat. "I knew you would come."

"What can you tell me?" I step inside his shop and perch on an empty stool. "What happened here tonight?"

"I've been told not to speak to you about this. They made it very clear." Now, he looks up at me, a sad smile pulling down the corners of his dark as night eyes. He shifts his shoulders inside his collared shirt, a nervous twitch he's had as long as I've known him.

"What do you mean?" I lean forward and frown. "Who did?"

"You cannot be here, son." This wobbling tone of voice is the same tone he used when he found me shivering inside this place the day my mother tossed me aside. It sends burning ice to the core of my bones. He never talks this way unless something is wrong.

"Did they threaten you?" I hold my body very still, as still as the lightbulb dangling overhead.

"I think you know the answer to that question." His cat lets out a sharp cry. He hunches back over and rubs his fingers into her gray fur. Cat hair lurches into the air with every stroke, spilling onto the thick layer already coating his pants. "I know, Tabby, I know. It has been a rough night."

"What's wrong with your cat?" I stand, and the stool topples with a *crash* from the rush of movement.

"Please go," he whispers. "Please don't make this worse."

"Did they hurt Tabby?"

He nods.

Red fills my eyes, blinding me as my canines ache for blood. "What did they do? Tell me, Ronan."

He jumps at the harsh clip of my words. I need to rein myself in, but sometimes it's hard to control my urge to rip the world to shreds, especially when that world is full of people who would hurt an innocent cat in order to intimidate an old man.

"They drank from her." When he looks up at me, tears stain his wrinkled cheeks. "They said I have to keep my mouth shut. Or we won't be safe here any longer. They'll take my blood one last time, and then I'll be dead."

The Coils is home to hundreds of humans scooped up from all throughout No Man's Land by the vampire gangs. There aren't that many humans left in the world, but Nightshade and Blackthorn managed to find enough to start up a blood bank. The humans trapped inside this place are nothing but slaves, forced to give their blood every single week to the vampires. As long as they go along with it, they're protected. If not...well, then they're used up one last time and extinguished.

If they were here threatening Ronan, someone is covering their tracks. This is typical Nightshade behavior. Quietly, I bend over and right the stool before sitting back down. I close my eyes and take several deep, slow breaths. I must be calm. I must be still. The only way to avenge is by keeping a lid held tight on the sharpest things you feel. "You saw something they didn't want you to see."

He nods.

"I'll take care of everything. Just tell me what happened."

"I can't." He holds the cat tighter to his chest. "You know I can't."

I'm not going to get anything more from him. The Nightshade crew behind this made certain of that.

"Come with me. To my house," I say. He once took me under his wing when I needed it the most. It's time I repaid the favor.

"My home is here. I won't have them scare me away." He runs his hand across the top of his thinning head of hair and glances around at his shop. It's been here for years, for as long as I can remember. When he took me in for those twelve months I spent lost inside these streets, I helped him hang his amulets on the wall every Monday night, color-coded from darkest to lightest. He'd give me a ball of yarn as reward, and then I'd sprawl on the dusty floor to play with the slum cats for hours.

"And it's not just me. It's everyone on Bright Street. I can't abandon them. We must stick together, us blood bank humans. But you should take Tabby." He stares down at his cat, ruffling her fur with his fingers. His frown is so etched into his face, it seems like a permanent scar.

"All right." I sigh. "Have it your way and stay. I'll take the cat."

"You will keep her safe for me?"

"I will not only keep her safe." I stand and loom over him with a new sense of purpose. One I haven't felt since the day I first decided to turn my nighttime self into a vicious copy of me. "I will find out who is threatening you. And I will make them pay."

CHAPTER 4
GWEN

I push my motorbike to full throttle on my way home, and Downtown and the Coils fade into tiny specks in the rearview mirror. The adrenaline high was like an egg—all the goo inside the fuel for kicking ass. But now all that goo has been scrambled, gobbled up, digested. All I have left is a useless shell. A shower and sweatpants are needed immediately. My father's okay, though, and that's all that matters.

I won't think about the other thing that happened tonight. Meeting Orpheus. I scowl as his chiseled face, broad shoulders, and massive biceps fill my mind. When I looked into his midnight eyes, something inside of me tugged me toward him. He's my fucking mate. Does the universe have a cruel sense of humor? It must.

I slow just before hitting the edge of a quiet, little Uptown neighborhood on the waterfront called Royal Hill. Our shared building squats right in the dead zone, before the empty office buildings are swapped out with the rows of historical brownstones. It's four stories, steel, and ridiculously ugly. Something about it reminds me of a clump of staples. But it's out of the way of literally everything else, making it the perfect place to hide the truth of what we do at night. So, whatever works, I guess.

The motorbike rattles while I idle outside the garage door and poke the security number into the keypad my father attached to the dashboard. Paranoia and my dad are best friends. Because of that, there's a different security code for almost every door in this building, including the ground floor garage.

After parking the bike, I crawl inside the elevator that leads to the rest of the building and slouch against the wall. There were a lot of things I expected for my first hands-on fight. Bruises: check. Swollen knuckles: check. Honor and glory: fail. I'm going to have to get over my little (or maybe not so little) slums anxiety problem because next time I might not have luck on my side.

The elevator dings when it reaches my floor, and I pad into the dark apartment. Before doing anything else, I zero in on the little decorative table by the door. I squat down and scoop the burner phone from its hidden harness on the underside. No calls, no messages. My father hasn't checked in yet. Weird.

An hour later, I've scrubbed my skin clean with scalding water and coconut body wash, climbed into warm sweats, and checked the phone a gazillion times. Still no message. If my father is working with the Saints, he would follow his OCD protocol to send me a coded message on this burner phone. But he hasn't. I pace back and forth across the hardwood floor by the foot of my bed. There's no way he's actually in trouble with them. The Saints would never harm one of their own.

Would they?

Sighing, I pace out of my room and down the short hallway to the staircase leading up to the next apartment. When I reach the door, I take a deep breath before banging out a knock so loud my ears ring. A few moments tick by before the door cracks open.

Kole stares at me through half-lidded eyes, his ginger hair bunched into tiny, cresting waves. "Do you know what time it is?"

"Hey, Kole." I sag against the doorframe.

"You sound funny. What's wrong?"

It's eerie how he can read me from two words and a sag, even when he's at least eighty percent asleep. "Come downstairs?"

"Yeah, give me five." He disappears behind the door, and I drag myself back down the stairs to wait for him in my living room. I ease onto the leather sofa and stare out the window at the dark skyline. When the Saints showed up tonight, I'd instantly relaxed. Dad came out of the Coils safe and sound, and the vampires were gone.

They wanted to question him, but that's not the first time they've taken him to their cathedral. Most of the time, they just want to know what's going on in this hellscape of a city.

Kole shuffles into the living room. He wears a smile and pale orange shirt that matches his eyes. His ears are sharp and pointed at the top, signalling his fae heritage. I lift my feet to give him room on the couch, and then plop them onto his lap after he sits. Having Kole in the building is one of the few things stopping me from failing Sanity 101. He's my best friend, my brother, even if not by blood, and the only person in the world who knows every single one of my secrets.

He grins and holds out a bottle. "Beer. You look like you need a drink."

"Fuck yes."

He flicks the cap off his beer with a pop and hands me the bottle opener. Eyeing the miniature trash can across the room, he launches the cap in the air. It hits the scuffed wall in the same place as always with a *clink* and drops right in without even touching the rim.

"I can't believe you found some more beer. The city's been low on it for years." I take the opener and jumble it around until I've popped the cap. Steam swirls from the open top, and I take a gulp of the bitter drink. Not exactly what I'd call tasty, but the warmth in my belly is exactly what I need after the sky dumping buckets on me. "What did you have to trade for this?"

"Nothing. Eric and Elliott got it for me." He smiles and dimples dot his cheeks, even though his face is all angles—cheekbones, chin, and forehead.

"Nice. I'll make sure to thank them next time I see them."

He takes another sip of his beer. "So, are you going to tell me why you woke me up at whatever ungodly hour this is?"

"Dad took me out again tonight. For a training sesh." Kole's presence momentarily distracted me from obsessing over the burner phone, but now my eyes flick back to the screen. Still nothing.

"Color me surprised." The leather couch crinkles as he leans back and laces his hands behind his head. "Gwen, when you and your dad both disappear around midnight, I usually assume you're not going out for groceries."

"Well, it's worse than what you think." My eyes drift away from Kole, past the TV, and to the only decoration on the living room walls. A framed, black-and-white photo of Towton City at its prime in 1982, before the vampires started screwing it all up. Before the slums were a blood bank, before all the Houses descended into a bloody war. We've been picking up the pieces ever since, out here in No Man's Land. The Houses have their truce. We have none of that.

I could leave, of course. Join a House. Go back through the

portal to the angel world. But…I can't leave this city. These people need help.

Kole twists sideways and wraps his fingers around my hand still clutching the phone. I lean my head against the back of the couch and meet his eyes, the tension in my shoulders packing up and going home. We sit in silence, just staring at each other. I don't need to say a word for Kole to know my mind is like a storm cloud.

"What happened, Gwen?" he finally asks.

I take a deep breath and dive into the explanation. The scream. The vampires in ski masks. The fight where I kicked at least a little bit of Nightshade ass. When I get to the part about the slums, Kole holds up his hands to stop me.

"You didn't follow them in there, did you?" His frown is a mirror image of what I feel inside.

"No. I tried, but then I had a panic attack. It was a barrel of laughs."

"I thought you didn't have those anymore."

"I don't." I shake my head, and wispy strands of dark hair fall in my eyes. "This is the first time in over a year."

I take a long gulp of beer and try to ignore the way Kole is watching me. Whatever happened in the past is done. I don't need pity from him or anyone else because of it. Still, he did see me when I was fifty feet under rock bottom, and I can't blame him for thinking the panic attack is bad news.

"Are they coming back?" he asks quietly.

"I don't think so," I say. "I'm pretty sure it was just getting close to the slums that triggered it."

"That would do it."

My fingers fidget and pull at the label on my barely-touched beer. I have the sudden urge to change the subject to something else, to anything at all. Talking about panic attacks makes my skin itch and my ears ring, sensations that are way too much like the real thing.

"Right about the time I felt like I was going to pass out, that freaking Orpheus guy popped out of nowhere." There, subject changed.

Kole straightens. His eyes widen, and he rubs his hands together as if he's just been given another stack of beer. Before tonight, I might have reacted the exact same way. Orpheus is something of an enigma. No one really gets who he is and what he stands for, and for months, I've been dying to puzzle it out. The stories paint him as a cold, calculating, and malicious killer. The fact he acted the total opposite tonight still has me weirded out.

That, and you know, the fact *he is my fucking mate*.

"Spill the tea, Gwen," Kole says eagerly.

"There's not much to say. He was an asshole and called me delusional." Just the memory of his words makes my teeth grind together.

Kole raises his eyebrows. "Does he look like the pictures?"

"He's bigger. Massive muscles." I frown. "And I...well, this is hard to say. I got this feeling in my gut when I looked at him. That he's my mate."

A beat passes in silence. "Wait a minute. Are you saying that Orpheus, the assassin, is your *fated mate*?"

I wince. "Yeah, but it's not like I'm going to do anything about it. Who needs a fated mate anyway?"

"Um. Gwen."

"*Anyway*, I didn't have to deal with him for long because the Saints showed up. Dad came out of the Coils, and he left with them." I hold up the burner phone. "No messages though. I'm kind of worried."

"This is the first time you've seen him out there." He nods at the floor-length window that gives us an unobstructed view of the northern parts of the city. "Doing his thing, you know? I'm sure there's an explanation. It probably has to do with those vampires who jumped you. Maybe they're mixed up in angel feather trade, and the Saints wanted to ask your dad about it. I don't think we need to worry."

"But you know how Dad is. He always sticks to protocol. What if he's actually in trouble with them?"

"If something's happened, they'll clear it up soon." Kole tips back his beer to swallow the last drops. "Everyone knows he'd never do anything wrong, especially not to another angel."

"Yeah. You're probably right." I finally release my cling-film grip on the phone and set it on the floor by the couch. Following Kole's lead, I guzzle the beer and wipe my mouth with the back of my hand.

"We could always call them and ask," he says.

"That would *really* be against protocol."

Go home and sit by the burner phone, Gwen. Don't do anything at all except wait, Gwen.

More and more I'm thinking protocol sucks.

A HIGH-PITCHED WAIL jolts me awake. My cell phone shrieks from across the room. My cell phone. Not the burner phone, I barely register. Heart lurching in my chest, I hurl myself out of bed and my feet twist up in the sheets. My bruised knees slam into the floor. *Eurgh.* I scrabble over to my desk, squinting my eyes at the sun slanting in through the windows.

"Dad?" I ask without even glancing at the caller ID.

"Gwen. Are you all right?" My father's familiar voice rumbles over the line. Sighing, I lean my back against the wall and smile.

"Yeah, I'm fine. Where the fuck are you?"

"I need you to stay calm." Those words do the exact opposite to my emotional state. I press away from the wall and start pacing back and forth at the foot of my bed and ignore the throbbing headache squatting on my eyeballs. "There are four things I need to tell you. One is that the Saints have decided to keep me for awhile, and right now I'm in their dungeon. Two—"

"Wait, what? Why?" I bite my tongue to keep questions about last night from spilling out of my mouth. "You're *in their dungeon*?!"

"Listen to me. *Two*, you need to stay out of this. Don't do anything stupid. You aren't nine anymore. You need to be responsible. Four, go to your job today and don't miss any of your seven working hours."

"I'm sorry, what? I don't understand what's going on." My head spins. He's talking complete nonsense. Dungeons, nine years old, my job. Hell, I don't even *work* seven hour shifts. "Why do the Saints have you? Why aren't they letting you leave? What *happened?*"

"No time to discuss. Limited phone privileges." He clears his throat. "Don't do anything stupid. Do you understand what I'm trying to tell you?"

"No, I don't understand!"

The dial tone blares in my ear before I get another word in edgewise.

CHAPTER 5

SILAS

I don't know why I torment myself by going Uptown so often. Every noise scrapes against my eardrums as I move down the sidewalk. Store doors swing open as supernaturals stream out with shopping bags. Knives and forks clatter from a nearby restaurant. There is nowhere to hide, unlike the nighttime alleys I frequent more often than this busy street.

Even though the city is mostly a vampire hellscape, fae and shifters and angels have carved out a decent existence for themselves. No one bothers anyone else. The supernaturals who aren't in the gangs look the other way, letting the vampires carry on with whatever they want. We have no authorities here. No laws. No rules. As long as you're left alone, you don't really care. Especially when it comes to the Coils and the humans who are trapped there.

I shove in to a pub called The Red Hammer. Inside, my eyes adjust to the dim lighting. Even though this is a den for all supernaturals, it screams vampires with its red velvet booths and gothic chandeliers. I spot Blain Shade in the back corner. He's the sole reason I came here today. As always, he has a girl by his side. A petite blonde who is a stranger to me. Another victim of his charms, no doubt. The lopsided smile and the dark hair slicing across his fire-red eyes seem to create a magnet for anyone with breasts.

I need to get rid of his newest conquest so that Blain and I can have a nice chat. He may be more separated from the vampire gang world than I am, but he's the nephew of Nightshade's current leader. He has access to inside information, even if he never uses it. The only problem with this plot, of course, is that Blain tends to glare in my general direction whenever I'm near. If he could froth at the mouth, he would.

The double doors behind the bar open. I look up. Gwen Kane strides in from the kitchen with several wine bottles, pinned in on either side by Kole Mason and Elliott Edwards. Their trio is a strange one. Kole is a sporty fae, tall and thin as a blade. Elliott is hard to pin down. She wears pearls and wide-rimmed black glasses, and she goes knocking on doors, trying to convince other supernaturals to care about the Coils. From her scent, I'm pretty sure she's a shifter, though I don't know which kind.

And Gwen? Well. Gwen is just Gwen.

She scans the booths and stills when her eyes settle on me. I meet her gaze, unblinking. There are remnants of last night written on her skin. Eyes ringed with purple stains. Knuckles swollen and tinged with red. She's wearing black jeans and a tiny little crop top that shows off her curves. Her words still echo in my ears. *You're a murderer.*

Her lips twist into something like a half-smile, half-frown. Fire sparks in her eyes, and she strides toward me, leaving Kole and Elliott behind the bar in a cloud of her exhaust fumes. I've seen that look before, but never directed at me. I did nothing last night to give me away, but there's a certain sense of purpose in the way Gwen Kane moves.

The thing is, she won't know I'm Orpheus. I wear an amulet around my neck during daylight hours. It not only protects me from full sunlight, but it also holds a glamor. A face that isn't mine. One she has seen a hundred times before.

It's the face everyone associates with Silas Thorn, but it's just as fake as my smile. It also means she doesn't see me as her mate when she looks at me.

"Hi, Silas." She stops in front of me, her long dark hair spilling over her shoulders. "How's everything going with your family?"

I raise my eyebrows and try to speak slightly deeper than I did last night, hoping she won't make the connection. "I haven't spoken to the Blackthorn vampires in years."

"So, you never hear from them anymore?"

"I have nothing to do with that gang."

Ever since Phantom drove my mother out of the city, Gwen has checked in on me as a concerned citizen. *How are you, Silas?* she'll ask with a brilliant smile that's impossible to turn away. Sometimes it seems as if she doesn't want me to hold her father's actions against her, but most of the time it seems as if she just wants to pump me for information. After last night, it's clear which one of these is the case.

I sit in the nearest booth and fold my arms when she joins me. Before last night's accusations, I would have given her a break, but I don't have the patience to play games today. "What is it you're after, Gwen?"

"What makes you think I'm after something?"

"You never talk to me unless you want to know something." I lean forward and lower my voice. "The last time you approached me, you asked me if my mother's second-in-command was still in Towton."

"I was just curious." Those deep brown eyes of hers flick over me, and for once, it's as if she's studying me the way I study her. If she hadn't just seen me as Orpheus last night, I might not mind being under her scrutiny. But if she inspects me for even a moment too long, she might begin peeling back the layers and see exactly who I am beneath this mask of mediocrity.

The amulet doesn't entirely change my features. It makes my nose a little longer, my jaw a little thinner, my cheeks a little fuller, and my eyes a shade darker. It doesn't even get rid of my canines, and it certainly doesn't change my build. If she stares at me for too long, she'll see it's me.

"In a city full of fucked up vampires, you're one of the only ones who isn't a total dick." She cracks a smile.

"Touché." I arrange my lips into something resembling hers. "So, what's your question?"

She laughs and pushes her hair behind her ear, revealing an owl earring dangling against her neck. Funny, I didn't take her for the earring type. "Okay, you caught me. I did come over here to ask you something."

"And?"

Her face crumples, and the smiling, laughing, fire storm of a girl is no longer here. "My father was taken by the Saints last night, and I think it has something to do with Nightshade. I just wondered if you'd heard anything."

"Damian Kane taken by the Saints? For what?" I keep my face as blank as possible. Feigning ignorance is not my forte, but this is the rare situation that calls for it. Silas Thorn wouldn't know about Phantom. Only Orpheus does.

"I was hoping you could tell me."

"Gwen, you know I don't know anything."

She sighs and grabs a paper straw from the basket of condiments on the table. Frowning, she traces invisible circles on the wood. Her eyes flick up to me, wide, watery and streaked with red cobwebs. Inwardly, I groan. I'm toast against that face. All my resolutions to stay angry with Gwen now seem like a foggy, distant memory.

My fucking mate is in pain.

I reach across the table and take the straw from her fingers. "Breathe, Gwen."

"It happened inside the Coils," she says in a tumbling rush of words. "Don't you have friends who live in there? You could ask them if they've seen or heard something."

"That's not possible."

On the other side of the pub, Blain's conquest bobs back to the bar to make an order, leaving him alone. For now. If anyone here knows something about Phantom's arrest, it's him. And if Gwen grills him with a few questions of my own, I might be able to learn some information about Ronan's attacker.

"I have another idea," I say. "But it involves an exchange, so to speak."

Gwen leans forward. "You want to make a trade? I've got plenty of stuff. Angel feathers, obviously. But also shifter blood and fae hair. Or some beer? We don't have much here. Just wine and hard liquor. But I do have a few bottles of beer at home you could have."

"Not exactly. Did it occur to you that Blain over there would probably know more than I would?"

She cranes her neck to glance over her shoulder at Blain. When she twists back around, she sighs and shakes her head. "He's not going to know anything. He's not a member of the Nightshade gang."

"Neither am I. But that certainly doesn't stop you from interrogating me."

"You've always known the answers to my questions though, Silas." Her lips quirk into a smile. She's right. It seems she's paid more attention to my willingness to talk to her than I'd thought.

"Talk to Blain," I say. "See what he knows. And while you're at it, I have a few questions of my own."

"Really? What do *you* need from him?"

There's only so much I can reveal without completely giving myself away, but getting caught in a web of lies is what everyone else in this iniquitous hellhole does. Not me. "Someone in the Nightshade gang is threatening a friend of mine, I think."

"Of course they are." She frowns. "You can't ask Blain yourself?"

"I can. However, I highly doubt he'd share much with me." I shrugged and leaned back in my seat. "The last time we spoke, I broke his jaw. And his nose. It happened just outside this pub, in fact."

"Oh…right." Her eyes become more focused on me as she no doubt remembers that day. It had been a quintessential display of my vampire temper before I learned to control it. I haven't lost myself like that again, not since the moment Blain's blood splattered onto my skin. "What do you want me to ask him?"

"Try to find out if any of the Nightshade crews have been making unscheduled visits to the lower levels of the Coils." It wouldn't explain Phantom's involvement, but it would give me a direction to target my hunt.

"You don't think they'd do that, do you?" she asks. "They leave the humans alone except for their weekly scheduled blood donations."

"They don't give a shit, Gwen. They'll go in there when they want."

She leans forward and lowers her voice to a whisper. "Do I want to know what you're going to do with this information?"

"I don't know. Do you?" I curl my lips into a smirk, silently daring her to jump to the conclusion of who I am. We both lean back into the booth and eye each other, and it's clear we're both saying more than our words reveal.

"You should be careful. You know they're really dangerous. You may come from a powerful vampire family yourself, but—"

"I can take care of myself." If Gwen knew the things I've done, she'd be far more worried about my enemies than me.

"Fine," she says. "You said this was an exchange. What do I get?"

"If Blain doesn't know why the Saints took your father last night, I have another way to find out."

"Deal," she says without a moment's hesitation, and then pushes up from the table. "Wish me luck."

"Try not to piss him off." I stand and follow Gwen across the pub to Blain's corner.

When Gwen reaches his table, I slip over to the wall and slouch against it, pretending to find my cell phone much more engrossing than it really is. Blain's back is to me, but I'm close enough to overhear every word.

"Hey, Bly." Gwen opts for the nickname all the other girls use and drops into the seat across from him. "How's life?"

"Much better now that you're here. Been sitting here for a couple hours now, and you haven't come 'round to say hi."

"Oh." Gwen's pale cheeks darken to red. "I've been too busy. You know, working. These drinks don't serve themselves."

"You should never be too busy to come see me." His voice is as smooth as the barrel of a gun, and I fight the urge to join the conversation and put an end to this insufferable flirting. "So, how've you been?"

"To be honest, not so great." Gwen leans forward and eyes Blain's order of food before lifting one of his french fries. "My father's been taken by the Saints."

"That's odd. How come?"

"I don't know. No one is telling me what's going on." She crosses her legs and brushes her hair back from her shoulders before leaning in closer. "I hate to ask you this, but have you heard anything?"

Blain stiffens. "Why would *I* have heard something?"

Gwen sighs and flicks her eyes up at me. I shrug my shoulders. I'm not bailing her out of this one. She had a decent start, but the direct approach doesn't work with people who are used to passive aggressive manipulation.

"It has something to do with your…family," she says.

"My uncle might be in Nightshade, but I'm not actually part of that gang, you know." Blain's voice is low and gravelly, and even though I can't see his face, it's clear Gwen hit a nerve.

"I know," she says. "I just thought you might have heard something."

"Well, I haven't."

"Nothing at all? Even something about things going down in the slums?"

I still. All of the pubs's clanging and tittering falls to a background hush while I wait for Blain's next words.

He clears his throat. "I did hear something about that actually."

A ghost of a smile crosses Gwen's lips, but she's quick to shut it down. "What can you tell me?"

"Sounds like there might be another fight for which vampire gang controls the Coils, for the blood. They're having a meeting about it tonight at Four Points Pizzeria. Vincent and Layla were talking about it this morning when I stopped by to talk to my uncle."

This is not good news. Right now, Nightshade controls the Coils and the Blood Market—the actual supermarket where all the blood is sold. If Blackthorn is gunning to take over again, there'll be a war. The last time this happened, a lot of people died, including Gwen's mother. It's now even more essential I put an end to this as soon as possible. Once it begins, it'll be impossible to stop. And Ronan won't be the only innocent human caught in the crossfire.

"Don't ever ask me about Nightshade again," Blain says.

Gwen blinks. "I'm not going to apologize for trying to find out what happened to my father…" She trails off when Blain's conquest returns with two shots of whiskey. "Oh hey, Sarah. Sorry I'm in your seat."

Gwen stands and brushes past Sarah without giving Blain another glance. I press away from the wall and fall into step beside her.

"You get all that?" she asks.

"I did." I put my hand on the small of her back and steer her toward the front doors of the pub. I don't know why I do it, I just do. And she feels damn good beneath my fingers. "I also noticed you didn't take my advice about not pissing him off."

"I have a gift." Gwen glances up at me, eyes narrowed. "Where are you taking me?"

"We need to make a phone call." When we reach the exit, I hold open the door for Gwen, and she breezes through. I catch the scent of her shampoo. Something summery. Maybe coconuts. I take a moment to breathe her in, chest tightening.

For fuck's sake.

"Who are we calling?" she asks when I join her on the street.

"Just wait." I hold up a hand before dialing the familiar number.

The line on the other end picks up. "Saint's Cathedral. How may I help you?"

"I'm calling about Damian Kane." I frown at the silence that follows. On the other end, the angel shuffles some papers before clearing her throat.

"What would you like to know?" she finally asks.

"What have you brought him in for?" I pace halfway down the block, ignoring the intermittent blare of car horns. Gwen trails behind me.

The angel sighs. "Damian Kane is being held because we believe he murdered another angel. Named Nicholas Tanner."

Murder. Nicholas Tanner. I killed someone named Nicholas Tanner. At least, that was what the ID said. But he was a vampire. He had fangs. *Fuck.* I suck in a breath and put my palm flat against the nearest building to steady myself. The cars and people streaming by form blurry puddles of orange and beige.

What the hell is going on?

CHAPTER 6
GWEN

"Silas. I need you to talk to me." Goosebumps stampede my arms, and I yank him around to face me. He looks at me through slitted eyes as he slides the cell into his black leather jacket pocket.

"Stop stalling. Tell me now, Silas."

"Promise you won't fly off the handle."

"No." I lift my chin and take a step closer, staring into his impossibly dark eyes. Normally, I feel like I could get lost in those eyes, but not right now. "I refuse to promise that."

"Fair enough, but I shouldn't be the one to tell you this." He clears his throat. "Gwen, the Saints are holding him for murder. Of another angel."

The ground drops out from under me. I blink at Silas and shake my head so hard my neck screams at me to stop. His words don't even make a microscopic sliver of sense. *Murder?* How can my dad be held for murder? Everyone knows Phantom doesn't kill. This can't be right. It *has* to be a mistake.

And he definitely wouldn't be dumb enough to kill an angel,

not with the Saints running around.

"My father isn't a murderer." My thunderous voice bounces off the buildings around us, though it's quickly drowned out by the cars that rumble by.

"This is an unlikely turn of events, I'll give you that."

"An *unlikely turn of events?*" I spit the words back at him and fist my hands. My voice rises another octave. "I'll tell you what an unlikely turn of events is, and that's a bunch of fucking angels not getting the shit beat out of them for this."

"Gwen, look at me." He slides a finger under my chin and forces me to look up. "Look at me."

I squirm, but I do what he says. I look at him, at his strong jaw, and his high cheekbones, and his eyes. They're the color of the darkest sky, and they look so, so familiar. Something about them makes the urge to throttle something a little less intense. Though if someone plopped a punching bag in front of me right now, I wouldn't argue.

"Punching a member of the Saints isn't going to solve anything. In fact, it'll make it worse."

"Well, I have to do something."

He raises his eyebrows. "Punching me also won't solve anything."

"This isn't a joke, Silas."

"I know. Do you have all your things with you?"

"My things?"

"We'll go talk to them. In person. See what they can tell us. The Saints are assholes, but they won't do anything rash without proof."

"Proof? There can't be any proof. My dad didn't kill anyone." A scream lodges in my throat, and I swallow it back. It's as if I'm a stick that someone just stomped on, and at any second, I'll snap in two.

"Don't forget where we live." Silas screws his lips into a twisted smile, but it's clear there's no humor behind it. "Towton City, the capitol of violence, corruption, and betrayal, under no House, protected by no one but ourselves. Welcome to No Man's Land."

"What are you saying?"

"Maybe someone's being paid by one of the vampire gangs to be a false witness. It would get Phantom off the streets and make their lives easier," Silas says. "Whoever actually made the kill certainly isn't involved."

"What makes you think that?" I cock my head and narrow my eyes. Sometimes Silas patches his words together in such a way that it sounds as if there's a bigger meaning behind them. Maybe it's just the way he talks, or maybe there's more to him than meets the eye. For two years, while I've worked at this bar, I've tried to solve the Silas puzzle. He comes by a lot. And for two years, I've shoved mismatched pieces together with none of them pairing up to form an actual clue as to what makes him tick.

"Trust me. I just know." He nods toward the street. "You ready to go?"

"Thanks for the help, but you don't have to tag along." The Silas puzzle will have to wait another day. As always, there's a bigger problem barreling down on me.

I twist on my heels and stride toward the parking lot behind the building. Now that I have a plan, the raging fire in my belly has calmed to a flickering flame. All I have to do is find out the names of any so-called witnesses. And everything the gang is paying them, I'll pay them double. No, I'll pay them *triple*. Whatever it takes to clear my dad's name and get the Saints to let him go.

"No, I'm coming." Silas matches my pace and falls into step beside me. "Moral support. You'll need it."

I pause at the street corner, frowning. Silas is the last person I'd expect to offer me *moral support*, but the truth is, today is turning out to be that kind of day. "Suit yourself."

We continue forward into the blustery day, burdened by dark clouds scudding across an iron sky. Last night's storm brought a fresh burst of frost, and the ground crunches beneath our shoes as we trot down a set of stairs and into the underground parking lot.

We reach my black motorbike, and I grab my helmet from the back before hopping onto the seat. Silas stands with his hands shrugged into his pockets and a frown pulling at his already downturned lips.

"Sorry, I don't have an extra helmet with me," I say. "At least we don't have to go far."

"You expect me to ride on that with you?" For the first time since I met Silas Thorn, he's letting me see a crack in those indestructible walls he builds around himself. He's not a fan of motorcycles, it seems. I bite back a smile.

"Or you could stay here," I say.

"No chance."

Silas hops onto the back of the bike without any warning. The added weight almost knocks me off-balance, and I throw out my legs to stop us from splatting onto the ground.

"Don't worry. I'm a good driver." I yank on my helmet and crank the engine. The motorcycle roars to life, humming that familiar song of pent-up energy and speed. Silas yells something at my head, but the eruption of noise muffles his words. With another crank of the engine, I throw the bike forward and whip out of the parking lot.

Silas finds my waist with his hands. Hot blood rushes into my cheeks, even with a storm of frozen air whipping around us. I've never had a guy other than Kole ride on the back of my bike. It's distracting to have his hands on my waist and his steady warmth consuming me. My fingers curl tighter around the handlebars, and I force my focus on the road. The way Silas touches me isn't important right now. All that matters is helping my father.

But, I have to admit…I don't entirely hate it.

In a record-breaking five minutes, I reach the headquarters of the Saints, housed in an old cathedral, and angle my bike into an open spot around the corner. As I shake my hair out of my helmet, Silas's hands stiffen around my waist. Heart pounding, I glance over my shoulder at him. His eyes are like fire.

I clear my throat.

"Has anyone ever told you that you drive like a maniac?" He releases his grip on me, climbs off, and watches me prop the bike on its kickstand.

"Just come on." I run around the corner and up the wide, curving steps with Silas trailing behind. Dodging towering white pillars, I reach the front doors and throw myself inside.

Our shoes click on the marbled floors as we cross the entrance of the cathedral. Overhead, elaborate paintings of past supernatural wars spread across the domed ceiling held up by a scattering of twisting pillars. Through another set of doors, rows of velvet-topped seats face an empty dais.

A glossy-haired angel clears her throat and walks toward us. Her white wings flare out behind her, matching her dress. Unlike my father, the Saints tend to show their wings most of the time.

"How can I help you two?" she asks in a soft voice that echoes in this cavernous room.

"I'm here to talk to someone about Damian Kane."

She frowns. "May I ask your name, please?"

"I'm Gwen Kane. His daughter."

"I see." She motions to a bench that sits in the corner. "Please wait over there, and someone will be with you in a moment."

She vanishes through the doors before I have a chance to ask anything else. With a sigh, I move toward the bench. Silas falls in beside me. I stare hard at the marbled floors, as if the swirling pattern will show me the solution to saving my dad from this mess, but the multi-colored lines are just as disjointed as my thoughts are.

"I know what this is like, you know. Wondering what's happening to a family member," Silas says. "Even though she's a horrible person, Isolde Thorn is still my mother."

I glance at Silas, eyebrows raised. "You've always given me the impression that you're glad my dad ran her out of town."

"Oh, don't get me wrong." Silas twists to face me and drapes one arm across the back of the bench. I try not to notice how close he is, how impossibly large his bicep looks against the wood. "I am *ecstatic* she's no longer here. But I still had to deal with all that, plus the possibility that she wouldn't survive in No Man's Land alone. You probably think she shouldn't survive. To be honest, I do, too, but it took me a long time to accept that."

"I wouldn't wish death on anyone," I say. "It's not up to us to decide who lives or dies."

Silas flicks his eyes away. "We'll have to agree to disagree on that one, Gwen Kane."

Frowning, I open my mouth to argue, but the click of shoes snags my attention away from Silas. I turn to see Alaric, one of the angels, walking toward me. He wears a black ensemble and a sword strapped to his back, and his wings are nowhere to be seen. Even though his sideburns and the short wisps of hair around his ears are tinged with white, his smooth face and bright eyes stop him from looking a day over thirty.

"Alaric." I hop up from the bench. "What's going on with my father? Is he all right?"

"He's fine, Gwen," he says, running a hand through his hair.

"But we're not happy about what he did. An angel named Nicky Tanner is dead. He's no one we know, but that doesn't matter. Angels are off limits. No one's allowed to kill one of us, not even Damian Kane."

"He didn't murder anyone, Alaric. Surely you know that."

He winces. "Evidence suggests otherwise."

"What evidence? Do you have witnesses?"

Alaric just glances away.

"I want to see him," I say in a low voice. "Let me talk to him."

"Not possible."

My fingernails carve half-moons into my palms as I crush my hands into fists. In the past twelve hours, the world has conspired to drop me onto a runaway train headed straight toward a yawning cliff. All I want is to stomp on the brakes, but every second brings me closer and closer to hurtling into the abyss. Silas places a hand on my elbow and squeezes twice. He's on my side, as strange as that is.

"You've got to give me something, Alaric. It's not fair to keep me in the dark like this. He's my father."

He nods and flicks his gaze around the empty cathedral. "All right. You can have something, but then you have to go. We have a witness. A woman called Layla. She says she saw your father murder an angel in the streets near the Coils."

I shake my head. "She's lying. It's not true. One of the vampire gangs is probably paying her to say this."

Silas edges in beside me and clears his throat. "This supernatural who died, are you sure he's an angel? Because I know of a vampire named Nicky Tanner who's part of the Nightshade gang."

Hope flares in my chest, but Alaric's eyes frost over when he turns to Silas. "Isolde Thorn's son. You should stay out of this."

"I'm here for Gwen." Silas folds his arms. "Now, are you sure or not?"

"We have the body. He's an angel."

I frown. "But it's a strange coincidence, isn't it? You don't actually know this angel. Maybe Silas is right and—"

"He's an angel. I'm sorry, Gwen. You know our rules. No one kills one of us and gets away with it, even if we don't know him. I don't care what his fucking name is. Now, we'll look into things and make sure this witness isn't lying. But it doesn't look good."

Without another word, Alaric turns to go. I watch his smooth stride until he disappears from view, and with him, my last shred of hope. Shoulders sagging, I drag myself through the front doors and drop down on the steps outside. The bitter cold bites at my cheeks.

"Are you all right?" Silas asks.

"No."

He sits down beside me and glances up at the sky. "You know what I like about you Gwen? There's no bullshit. Whatever you're thinking just pops right out of that mouth of yours."

Something in me warmed.

"Did you feel like this?" I twist to face him, my fingers digging into the stone. "When your mother disappeared?"

"I'm not sure I know how you feel." His tone is softer than it usually is, almost too soft to hear over the rumble of a passing bus.

"Completely helpless," I say. "Like I have no control over anything happening in my life."

"I've felt that way before." A breeze ruffles his dark hair, and there it is again. That flash of something familiar. "A very long time ago."

"How did you get over it?"

Silas sits silent for a moment and stares up at the sky as if he's weighing his words on the heavy clouds. "I decided to take what was out of my control and put it into my control. Destroy the helplessness."

"But the problem is I can't destroy it. There are at least a dozen Saints and only one of me. And I'm not even a full angel."

"There's one thing I can say about the Saints. They can be fair, especially to their own kind. You just need proof the witness is lying." Silas meets my eyes, and a sharp glint reflects in the black of them. Whether it's from the blanketed sun or something deeper is impossible to tell. "And we have her name."

"Layla? Yeah, but I don't know who that is."

"She owns Four Points Pizzeria. I'm sure that rings a bell."

I straighten. "That's where a Nightshade meeting is happening tonight. About the slums."

"Exactly."

"I need to go." I hop up from the steps as if I've been injected with a gallon of VitaBrew, a special witch's concoction that's even more powerful than coffee. "Do you need a lift back to the pub?"

"I've had enough boozing for the day. I'll take the metro home." He stands and slips his hands into his pockets.

"You didn't even have one drink."

"I got distracted." He smirks.

"Right." Cheeks heating, I clear my throat and trot backward down the stairs. "Thanks for your help today."

"Anytime, Gwen Kane."

At that, I turn and take the steps two at a time. Silas said to destroy the helplessness, and the best way to do that is to destroy the one person standing between my father and his freedom. The false witness. If Layla wants shifter blood or fae hair or anything at all to change her tune, I'll give it to her. But if that doesn't work, I have something even better. My fists.

CHAPTER 7
SILAS

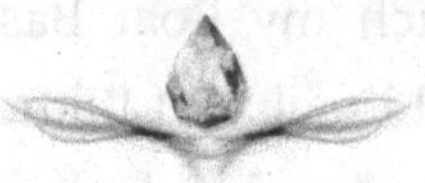

Gwen bounces down the steps, her hips swaying the way they did beneath my hands when she curved around the street corners on that motorcycle of hers. It will take me a good hour to get home from here, but I can't handle another trip on the back of Gwen's bike with her coconut hair streaming out of her helmet and tickling my nose. I came far too close to telling her the truth about everything, including who and what I am. *Orpheus. Her mate.* Now, she has what she needs, and I have what I need. It's time we part ways. It's the best thing for both of us.

I never should have encouraged her to talk to Layla. There's no question in my mind she'll beat down the doors of Four Points Pizzeria tonight, a pointless mission even if she's successful in getting inside. Because I can't let Gwen find out who really killed Nicky Tanner. I'm not an angel. The Saints would just execute me, no questions asked. No evidence or witnesses necessary. Plus, Nicky Tanner wasn't an angel when I killed him. He was a vampire. None of this makes any sense.

It might not even be the same person, but it's too much of a coincidence to ignore.

I need to speak to Layla before Gwen does.

I spend the next hour on the metro's stuttering Blue Line, my seat a stained plastic bench. There's a steady buzz from the flickering fluorescent bulbs that should have been replaced a dozen years ago. The vampire beside me reeks of cigarettes and blood, and by the time we reach my Boat Basin stop, the stench has soaked into my skin, and I feel as if I'll never get clean.

When I finally reach my tiny home on the river, the dingy boathouse is a welcome sight. After cutting off all ties with my family, I moved into the Boat Basin, a small residential dock with twenty or so rotting houseboats. It's part of a thin strip of land on the edge of the Coils, north of Downtown but still south of Uptown. The gangs ignore its existence most of the time.

"Hello, Tabby cat," I call out as I slip into my boat and lock the sliding door. A weak meow drifts toward me from the den-kitchen combo, so I head over to the sink to refill her water bowl. She hobbles over to me, still recovering from the feeding. I squat and place the water in front of her while scratching the patchy hair on her neck. Tabby reminds me of one of Ronan's cats from when I lived with him that year in the slums. The cat's real name was Presto, but I called him Three. He only had three legs, but it didn't stop him from following me everywhere I went in the slums, even if that meant digging his claws into the cables as I climbed.

Leaving Tabby with her water, I stand before my living room wall. This floor-to-ceiling square is my designated space for dealing with the vampires of this city. A photographic hierarchy chart hangs over all the newspaper clippings and maps and random scribbles I've hoarded these past two years. Robert "Bobby" Shade, the kingpin of it all, squats at the very top. He took over Nightshade only a handful of years ago, and ever since the banishment of my mother, his power and reach has multiplied each year like the frothing city rats. He has total control of the Coils, which means he owns the entire blood supply, as well as the Blood Market that sells it all to the hundreds of vampires who call this city home.

I lean in and add Layla Pirelli's name and a question-mark off to the side. Layla has been on my list of known associates since I started looking into things. She owns the pizzeria where the Nightshade leaders like to hang around, drinking, smoking, and stuffing their faces at a table on the back veranda reserved only for them. She benefits from protection and a host of other perks without ever being sworn in as a full member of Nightshade. I'm not sure what kind of supernatural she is. Probably a witch.

But Layla must be getting something else out of this. Nightshade welcomes in a few members who aren't vampires. Mostly witches or fae. And helping them get Phantom off of the streets is a surefire way to get into their good graces.

"Silas?" A shrilly voice blares through my boat's thin walls, and a banging ensues. I cross the room and slide open the door to Mrs. Casey wiping her hands on a flowery apron, her graying hair sticking out in every direction like a wild bush. She's human, just like Ronan. Unlike him, she welcomed my offer to get her out of the Coils about ten years ago. She's lived next door ever since.

"Silas," she says with pursed lips. "No work today?"

Mrs. Casey thinks I have a job as a garbage collector. Close enough.

"Needed to stop home to feed Tabby."

"Hmph." She adjusts her glasses and looks me up and down. "Better take off that jacket. You'll need to change into something you don't mind getting ruined, you see."

"What's wrong this time, Mrs. Casey?" I slide off my leather jacket, hang it on the hook by the door, and push up the sleeves of my black shirt. Perhaps this time she'll have me clean her oven.

"My son and his new wife are visiting tomorrow, and I wanted to have a batch of my famous chocolate chip cookies ready for them." She holds up a pair of withered, shaking hands and frowns at them as if she's never seen them before. "But these hands. They just don't work for me anymore."

I raise my eyebrows. "You want me to bake some cookies?"

"If you wouldn't mind, Silas." She smiles a smile more genuine than any other I've ever seen. Her eyes dance, the whiskered lines around them stretching all the way down the side of her face, evidence of how much she's used this same expression all her life.

"No problem," I say. "But I don't see why my clothes will get ruined."

"Oh." A tinkling laugh escapes from her lips. "I dropped my bag of flour. Everything is covered in it."

Mrs. Casey's boat is the polar opposite of mine. Where my small collection of basic black furniture is uncluttered and arranged in a precise fashion, Mrs. Casey's monstrous collection of multi-colored junk is tossed about in random chaos. Once inside her boat, I step over a rusted bicycle and make my way past a tower of books to get into the kitchen. The blue and green checkered counters and floors hide under a thick layer of flour. Even the miniature blue refrigerator hasn't escaped the attack.

Mrs. Casey whirls around with a bright smile. She shoves a dusty paper into my hand and waves at a collection of ingredients scattered across the counter. "Here are the instructions and the ingredients. I trust you can manage?"

"Looks pretty straightforward," I say with a glance at the list. "I'll clean up the flour while I'm at it."

"You are such a dear." She unties her apron and tosses it onto the counter to join the rest of the mess. "What would I ever do without you?"

I honestly don't know, I think, but I don't dare say it aloud. Mrs. Casey suffers from health issues, but I don't know the details. All I know is it requires a lot of pills, and a lot of rest, and she shouldn't live on her own. She wants to treat her visiting son to some homemade cookies when it should be the other way around. I've never met the guy—a half-fae—but when I do, we'll have a nice chat. The threat of ever seeing me again will be enough for him to do what he should have done years ago and move his mother into his house in Mt. Ranier, which is part of the House of Blood and Beryl. She shouldn't have to live in No Man's Land.

Mrs. Casey shuffles off to her back bedroom for a nap, and I set to work on the cookies. Once I get a batch in the oven, I scrub the floors, the counters, and every other surface camouflaged by flour. When Mrs. Casey finally stumbles into the room rubbing sleep from her eyes, the cookies sit cooling and the kitchen shines spotless. It's unfortunate I can't say the same for the rest of her home.

"Oh, Silas," she says with a smile. "They smell wonderful. And oh, look at the kitchen."

"Is there anything else I can do?"

"No, no." She edges up to the counter and peers down at the cookies. "You've done enough. You should go do something fun for once. Take a girl to dinner."

"I don't know any girls I want to take to dinner," I say, but my mind rages against me. *Lies*, it says, the faint ghost of coconut teasing my nose.

"Well," she says, walking me to her sliding door. "You'll meet your mate someday. You're still young yet, especially for a vampire. Oh!"

Mrs. Casey grabs a cardboard box near the door and holds it out to me. "This came for you earlier."

"A box for me?" I frown. No one knows my Boat Basin address.

Taking the small, square box, I stare down at the return label. It holds only a name, no address. Isolde Thorn. Gritting my teeth, I dig my fingers into the cardboard and fight against the urge to shove the box into the wall and beat it to a pulp.

"Everything okay, Silas?" Mrs. Casey asks.

"Yeah, everything's fine." I slide open the door as calmly as I can. "Knock on my door anytime you need help."

Back in my boat, I drop the box onto my couch and step back. The timing of this package can't be a coincidence, and the thought leaves a dry, bitter taste in my mouth. Someone is playing a game with me, and I do *not* like games.

Stalling isn't the answer, though, so I grab some scissors and cut through the packing tape. Slowly, I open the box and stare down at the contents. My canines suddenly ache, but I bite it back down. Inside, a chunk of skin sits on a bed of blood. White feathers have been sprinkled on top. This can only be one thing. Nicky Tanner's skin. And there's a note.

Thank you, Silas. XO - Mother.

It's her handwriting, all sharp points and slanted lines. I hurl the box to the floor and kick it across the room so hard it smashes into the wall. My mother is behind all of this. I should have known. I don't know why and I don't know how, but as always, she's sucking me into her little games, tying me up with each calculated strip of her plan so that it's impossible for me to escape.

That settles it. Layla Pirelli is a walking dead woman. My mother wants Phantom to take the fall for the Nicky Tanner's murder? Well, she won't get it. I will *make* Layla go to the Saints and tell them she made the whole thing up. Not only will it bring my mother's game to a grinding halt, but it will give Gwen back her father.

I grab my gun from underneath my couch cushion, glare out at the river, and wait for darkness to fall.

CHAPTER 8
GWEN

The shopping bags weigh down my arms when I bustle back into my apartment. I drop the bags by the elevator doors and check the burner phone, just in case. A heavy anchor slips further down inside my belly when there are no missed calls, even though it's not exactly a surprise.

"Gwen, where the hell have you been?" Kole appears in the living room doorway with his hands raised high at his sides. Elliott's head peeps out by his waist, her eyes trained on my pile of shopping. She usually pops by after work for awhile.

"And why did you disappear earlier?" Ells asks. "With Silas Thorn?"

A slow grin spreads across Kole's face. "Yeah, seems suspicious."

"Hey, guys. Nice to see you, too." I kick off my boots and glance up at the clock mounted on the wall. It doesn't feel late, but it's edging close to five, and the sun is already poking at the horizon.

"Don't try to change the subject." Kole jogs a step back when

I cross the floor to the living room. He launches onto the couch, his pine tree legs overtaking the entire length, though that doesn't stop Elliott from joining him.

"It's not nearly as thrilling as whatever you've come up with, I'm sure." I take the recliner by the television and sink into the soft leather. "I left to talk to the Saints. Silas helped me out."

"Oh." Elliott leans back into the couch and tucks her feet underneath her like a cat. "Kole told me the Saints took him in? I hope it's okay that I know."

"I was going to tell you anyway, Ells."

Her lips drift into a soft smile that dimples her cheeks. Elliott has always been the heart of our little group, knocking on doors to convince the supernaturals of this city to actually *care* what's going on here. Kole is the laughter, the energy, the fun. And me? I think I'm just the brute force, but I don't mind. It's what I do best.

"Did you get to see your dad?" Kole asks.

"No." I flick my eyes away and stare at the blank, silent television screen. "They wouldn't let me."

"You can't be serious." Kole grabs a newspaper from the glass coffee table and rips out a page before crunching it into a ball. He launches it at the trash can where it hits the mark and falls in with a swish.

"I did get a little information, but they were pretty tight-lipped about the whole thing."

"And?" Elliott clasps her hands and leans forward.

I open my mouth, but then snap it shut when a rock lodges itself in my throat. Unshed tears burn my eyes like tiny flames. Saying it aloud means admitting it's real, but if I can't admit it to Kole and Elliott of all people, how can I ever admit it to myself?

"They believe he murdered an angel," I finally say, my voice as cracked as worn pavement in the summer heat. "And you know what they'll do…"

The words hang heavy in the air. No one says a word. Moments pass in silence before Kole shifts on the couch to make a Gwen-sized gap between him and Elliott.

"Come here."

Kole opens his arms, and I pad across the room to slump into the couch between my two best friends. I press my face against his chest and liberate all the tightly-wound knots barely holding me together. Breath shuddering, the tears leak out of my eyes and spill onto his t-shirt. His arms snake around my shoulders, and on my other side, Elliott brushes my hair off my wet cheeks.

"I know it doesn't seem like it right now, but this is going to be okay," Kole says into the top of my head. "No one goes after Damian Kane and gets away with it."

My fists swipe at my eyes, and I pull away. "Damn straight."

"What are you going to do?" Elliott plucks a tissue from her bag.

"I guess Alaric is going to make sure the witness isn't lying." I empty the entire contents of my nose into the tissue and launch it at the trash can. Unlike Kole, my shot falls short by at least a foot.

"I mean, what are *you* going to do?" Elliot gives me a smile laced with meaning. "If you know what I mean."

"No, I don't know what you mean." When I turn to face her, she's fiddling with her pearl necklace. Her fingers slide the beads back and forth along the string, trembling the way they do when she's nervous.

"Your father is Phantom," she says. "I've known awhile."

"I didn't tell her," Kole interjects.

"How did you find out? Does anyone else know?"

"My brother doesn't. Not sure about anyone else." The

beads slide back and forth on Elliott's necklace. Whoosh, whoosh, whoosh. "You remember when I used to have that stalker?"

"How could I forget?" Frowning, the image of Elliott's frightened face pops into my mind. It was only a year and a half ago when she showed up at my apartment that night gulping in breaths as if she had no lungs. A shifter with a scar zigzagging down the side of his face had been following her around, from work to home and then back again. He lurked in the shadows and watched her every move, every wide-eyed glance in his direction. A month later, Elliott said the shifter stopped. She never saw his face again. He just vanished.

"Your father overheard me talking to you about it. As I was leaving, he pulled me into his office and told me who he is. He said he'd take care of it for me. And he did."

"Why didn't you ever tell me?"

"I figured you were keeping it a secret because you wanted it to be a secret. I didn't want to bring it up unless you did."

"I kept it a secret because I thought Dad didn't want me to tell anyone." I grab another tissue from Elliott's bag and dab it around my puffy eyes. "So, how much do you know?"

"Mostly what everyone else knows about Phantom. Plus, I figured out he's training you. All those late nights you talk about, and the bruises on your hands."

"Oh, these old things?" I hold up my knuckles and frown at the purple and black welt from that guy's stone slab stomach. Even with my half-angel healing, they still look raw. Lesson learned. Next time I'll go for his face.

Elliott smiles, but the beads continue to whoosh back and forth. I frown. She's never been good at hiding her emotions, especially when something is wrong. Her eyes and her pearl-swiping hands always give her away.

"Ells." I grab her hands and pull them away from her necklace, forcing her to meet my eyes. "What's wrong?"

She sighs and leans into the couch. "Something's happening. I came over hoping your dad could help."

I grip her hands tighter. "Is the shifter stalker back?"

"No, it's not that. I've been getting these weird phone calls for about a month now." She takes a deep breath. "Threats to kill me if I don't stop talking to people about the Coils."

"Okay." I jump up from the couch and pace across the room. When I reach the television, I twist on my heels and pace back. Heat rushes into my face like a firestorm, and a pent-up energy aches to escape. My muscles beg me for a punching bag. Without one, the walls may lose their smooth white finish when I riddle them with jagged holes.

"Gwen?" Elliott asks in a small voice.

"Don't worry. I'll take care of it," I say, using the same words my dad must have used that night when he assured Elliott everything would turn out okay. Though I'm not as certain as he must have been.

"What are you going to do?"

"I don't know, but I'll figure it out." I stop pacing and try for a reassuring smile. "For now, you can stay here if you want. Eric, too. We've got plenty of room. I'll look into who made those calls. And…I'll take care of it."

"Oh, thank god, Gwen." She launches off the couch and wraps her arms around me. Over her shoulder, I gaze up at Kole. His slowly shaking head and dropped jaw says it all.

AFTER THE THREE of us share some ramen noodles for dinner, I head to my room with my newly-purchased supplies. Kole follows me inside and leans against the wall with crossed arms, watching me dump the shopping bags onto my tangled sheets.

"So." He cocks his head. "Honesty time. What are you really going to do?"

"Honesty time." I glance out the window at the city's darkness. "I have no idea. Someone is threatening Elliott. Someone is starting a fight for the slums. And someone is framing my dad for murder. I'm a good fighter, but I can't tackle three things at once."

"One at a time, then." Kole grabs a bag and tips the contents out on the bed. "I'm guessing you didn't go shopping for a new ballgown this afternoon."

I smile. Kole's right. One thing at a time. I'll start by taking care of dad's so-called witness, and then I can move on to helping Elliott. If these threats have been rolling in for over a month, it's unlikely much will happen overnight. Plus, she and her brother will be safe here.

We pour the rest of the shopping onto the bed, and I snatch up the most important purchase. A new pair of black leggings. These are thick and sturdy, and it'll take a hell of a lot more than a prickly pair of gloves to rip these bad boys to shreds.

"What are these?" Kole lifts a massive pair of black boots plastered in silver buckles.

I snatch them out of his hands and almost drop them from the unexpected weight. "Combat boots. With spikes in the heels for extra damage."

"You're going to look ridiculous."

"You mean badass."

"If you say so."

"Wait here." Grabbing the rest of the stuff I got from bartering today, I shuffle into my bathroom to prepare for tonight's mission.

First things first: the outfit. I pull on my new leggings and a pair of thick socks before shoving my feet into the boots. It doesn't matter what Kole says. With their silver buckles and thick soles, they look like something straight out of Underworld, and if that chick isn't badass, then I don't know who is. Next up is a loose black top, cropped just below my breasts, crafted from a breathy material that will be easy to move in. A hood dangles down the back, perfect for when I need to hide my face in shadows.

After I've swept my hair into a ponytail, I blink at the mirror. The woman staring back at me is a fiercer version of who I usually am, and that's exactly what I'm going for here.

Once I've donned a pair of black leather gloves, I kick open the bathroom door and stride into the room, stance wide and fists raised. Kole coughs and punches his hand against his chest, his eyebrows so high they could shoot up off his forehead.

"Well?" I ask.

"Okay, I take it back." A grin splits his lips. "You do look badass."

"Badass enough to take on a known associate of the Nightshade vampires?" I open my hands and fist them again, the leather gloves crunching.

"Badass enough to take on the entire gang."

"Good." The can of pepper spray is the final touch. I grab it from the bed and shove it into my waistband. "Because it might come to that."

CHAPTER 9
SILAS

The Four Points is like the nest of a four-headed dragon. Four territories converge on one Downtown square lined with an assortment of vampire-owned businesses. There's the barbers where the Boss and Soldiers alike go for their haircuts and shaves, and a side order of shifter blood. There's the butchers, a place I still haven't quite nailed down, but I'm certain the meat in the back isn't only pork and beef. There's also the laundromat. More supernatural blood trade and some alleged drugs. The magical kind.

Then there's Four Points Pizzeria. That place is clean. It's even been designated one of the best restaurants in the city. Vampires flock there nightly, but it's only the members of the Nightshade gang who have access to the back tables. Some witches and fae even frequent the place. No one really cares it belongs to the gang. That could be Towton City's motto.

No one cares about anyone but themselves.

It's only seven, but I'm already wearing my Orpheus face. My *real* face. I have a gun in my pocket and a knife on my belt. I lean against a brick building just at the edge of Four Points, hidden amongst the deepening shadows.

Further down the street, impatient supernaturals shiver in their overcoats and scarves while they wait to get inside. If you aren't a member of Nightshade, you can't reserve a table, so the wait is always backed up. In the summer, sometimes the line winds around the entire block, while the Boss and his Soldiers sit inside chuckling away at the inferior supernaturals.

A black sedan with tinted windows rolls to a stop outside the restaurant. The door opens, and Bobby Shade, the big Boss himself, glides out of the car. A thick, boxy vampire the shape of a garbage dumpster. The opposite of everything you think of when you imagine a vampire. His black hair glistens under the streetlamp, and his brown suit is the color of weak diner coffee. I finger the gun in my pocket. If only I could take a shot at him right here and now. But from this distance, I'm sure to miss, and it would only take two seconds for an entire horde of Soldiers to descend upon me. Besides, I'd rather rip off his head. It would be far more satisfying.

Three others follow. The Mad Hatter bounces out of the car with a devilish grin. Today's hat is a dark purple bowler which, according to his insufferable ukulele songs, means he's in the mood to start a fight. He ambles down the sidewalk like a wiry giraffe, all neck and legs. The other two vampires are fairly nondescript. Vincent Shade, the Boss's son, and a Soldier named Ivan. They have the same dark hair and muscular build and generic suit. The four vampires shift through the waiting crowd and disappear into the restaurant.

As soon as the door shuts behind them, I push away from the wall and walk down the block. In these early hours, I have to stay out of sight. While the city places Phantom on a skyscraper high pedestal, people hate me. I couldn't care less, though. I'm not about to spare the life of a monster in exchange for a positive reputation.

I round the corner just before reaching the pizzeria, with one eye on the windows. Past thin, red-and-white checkered curtains, packed tables of supernaturals enjoy their stone-baked pies under the dimmed atmospheric lights. Dark red liquid sloshes from glasses—wine or blood—and stains smiling lips. Laughter and the clink of dishes drifts out into the street. It's a light, tinkling sort of sound. Such a contradiction to the revolting iniquity bubbling under the floorboards.

When I reach the back edge of the building, I pause where the brick transforms into a black, wrought-iron fence consumed by vines of dead leaves. No more laughter and wine glass clinks at this end of the restaurant. Instead, the air fills with harsh voices, but I can't make out their words.

I slip a finger into the vines and push a branch aside a sliver of an inch. There are four tables here in the back under a canopy of heat lamps. One table houses Bobby Shade and his closest allies, leaning closely together and whispering with emphatic hand motions. The other three tables are full of Soldiers not speaking a word. Blain was right. They're having an important meeting tonight, and they're not joking around.

Near the restaurant's back door, I spot Layla Pirelli. My jaw ticks. She's younger than I remembered. Even with her light brown hair twisted up into a tight bun, she doesn't look more than twenty-five. Her eyes track every movement of the head table while her lips smash together into a hard line. Not the kind of expression you'd expect from someone who just won over the head of a vampire gang.

"Layla, come over here now." Bobby Shade's words leap out like a bark. "Explain yourself."

How odd. Why would she need to explain herself? I press my eye closer to the fence, but a rustle near my face makes me snap back. A suit-clad body shifts in front of the gap and blocks my view. Frowning, I back away from the fence. I don't dare create another fissure in the twisting branches, but I need to hear this conversation.

Pacing further down the block, I take in my options. The cast-iron fence strains against the heavy vines and trembles at the gusts of cool wind, so climbing gets a vote no. Just behind it, a long stretch of darkened apartments barrel into the bowels of Downtown, but the building directly adjacent overlooks the back veranda with two stories of dusty windows.

I walk past the building, pause, and then stride into the darkness of an alley. Slipping my hands into my pockets, I wait. The chilly breeze scoots discarded fliers down the empty sidewalk while a lone pigeon pecks at the yellow lines in the pavement. Flecks of ice begin to rain down from bloated clouds. The shadows remain still, meaning the street belongs to me.

With a running start, I jump toward the fire escape and snake my hands around the rusted bar. The ladder clatters to the ground, the noise as loud as gunfire. I slip my boots onto shaking rungs and climb as quickly and quietly as possible before crouching atop the second floor's grated platform. Again, I wait. Caution and patience go hand in hand with successful stalking. When no angry shouts or gunshots explode into the night air, I scale up to the next platform and peer inside the building.

The shadows creep across the floor like witch's fingers, but even under the canopy of darkness, it's clear this vacant room is home to no one. Only dust decorates the carpet. No furniture, no adornments on the yellowing walls. The window frame shudders against my touch, and within seconds, I'm inside the room brushing the dust off my hands.

The floorboards creak beneath my feet when I cross the room to reach the window overlooking the veranda. Down below, the meeting has escalated. Bobby Shade totters on his feet, flapping his hands at Layla and shouting words I can't hear through the double-glazed panes.

A strange seed of an idea sprouts inside my brain. Pulling my gun from my pocket, I tap the window with the barrel and squint my eye to aim. My lips twist into the only version of a smile I know. No trees, no bushes, no fences obscure the view from here to the veranda. With a proper long-ranged weapon and plenty of vampire bullets, I could end the Nightshade gang once and for all. And I know just where to get that kind of weapon.

A blur of black by the fence snags my attention. The figure pauses with a hand clasped to the wrought-iron fence, very close to where I was just standing. My breathing slows.

Her face is hidden by a dark hood, but when she shifts to peer through the fence, the lights glint across a pair of blood-red lips. I let out a long, slow whistle that shakes me to my core. If only we weren't working for opposite ends, I would head right back down that fire escape and tell her exactly who I am.

Silas? She'd smile when I gazed into the depths of those dark eyes. The Saints would release her father. She'd understand the reasons I kill. I'd tell her I'm her mate, and she'd smile at that, too. Everything would be different.

But, in Towton City, reality is always a polluted version of what it should be.

A *click* echoes in the silent room. I sigh and give an imperceptible shake of my head. Of course nothing can be simple. Slowly, I twist around, careful to keep my gun hidden behind me.

A generic Nightshade Soldier stands before me, gun trained

right at my head. When he sees my face, his eyebrows arch into his smooth, pale forehead.

"It's you." He strides closer, the floorboards creaking under his weight. "The Boss will want to see you."

"Wonderful. Bobby and I have never been properly acquainted."

"Don't fuck around." One step closer. He taps the gun onto my arm. "Just because he wants to see you doesn't mean I won't shoot you if you try anything."

"Isn't now a bad time? Looks like he's pretty busy dealing with this Layla situation."

"What do you know about it?" He narrows his eyes.

"She told the Saints that Phantom killed an angel. Good move, really. I'm sure she expects Bobby to reward her for getting Phantom off the streets." Behind my back, I drop my gun into the folds of my jacket pocket.

The Soldier laughs. "You're an idiot. You've got it all wrong."

"Interesting." I snake my hands out from behind my back.

The Soldier lifts his gun. Instinct takes over. I smash my fist against his wrist, and he emits a strangled yell. With his other hand, he digs his fingers into my forearm and drags me across the floor. My feet trip up on the carpet, but I rip away from my attacker just as a silenced shot rings out. The bullet smashes into the wall behind me.

"You missed," I say with as much venom in my voice as I can muster.

I kick out. My boot pounds into his stomach. He doubles over. I twist his thick hair in one hand and grab his neck with the other. Underneath my fingertips, his throat bobs. My canines ache to bite his flesh. But I won't. I won't do it. Not once will I let myself be like them. I dig my fingers into his neck instead, pressing against his airways.

He sputters for breath, but still manages to slam a fist into my face. The pain explodes in my cheek, and I lose my grip, giving him an opening to slither away from me. As he slowly stands, gasping for breath, I pull my gun from my pocket.

"You shouldn't have missed," I say.

I level the gun at his head and shoot.

CHAPTER 10
GWEN

My patience is wearing as thin as Towton City's reputation. The ice pellets plopping on my head mean it's high time to speed things up. Plus, a blister on my toe throbs with every step I take. *Great choice of shoes, Gwen.*

I walk to the other end of the fence to try another viewpoint, but these vines are so thick, it's impossible to see what's happening inside the restaurant. A door suddenly swings open in the building just behind me. I dodge behind a utility pole, not that it'll do me much good.

Like a towering statue of pure stone muscle, Orpheus appears in the doorway. He backs out of the building slowly, dragging…a body. He's dragging a fucking body.

"Fancy seeing you here," he says with his back still to me.

He can't really be my mate. Right?

But there is no denying the instinctual pull, the intense need to reach out and touch his cheek. He's the opposite of me in every way, and yet it feels like he's the only place I could ever truly be home. Stupid fated mates bond. It's infuriating, to say the least.

"Orpheus. Again." I drag my eyes away from his impressive back and curl my hands into fists. "Are you stalking me or something?"

"I could ask you the same thing. I was here first." He pauses in his body dragging exercise. "Mind giving me some help here?"

A bitter laugh pops from my throat. "Help you dispose of a body? When hell freezes over. Who have you killed this time?"

"Some random Nightshade Soldier." With a shrug, he hooks his arms under the guy's armpits and resumes the slow march into the middle of the street.

A part of me wants to fight him for what he's done, but another part whispers a shout of victory. Another Nightshade vampire is off the streets. The innocents of the city can sleep a little safer. There are just *so* many other ways this could have been accomplished without stealing someone's life away.

"Did you really have to kill him?" I ask.

"In this case, definitely. He was either going to shoot me or take me to the Boss. Neither of those options appeal to me." Orpheus reaches the line in the middle of the street and drops the Soldier. With vigorous hands, he brushes at his entire jacket.

"I don't think he's contagious," I say with raised eyebrows.

"You'd be surprised."

"If you didn't want to touch him, then why bother dragging him into the middle of the street?" The ice pellets continue to fall, and I pull my hood lower over my face, thankful for the appropriate attire tonight. My stomach is a little cold, though.

"I'm not trying to hide anything. The faster he's found, the faster Nightshade knows I'm still out here. No matter what they throw at me." He nods at the building. "Though, in this case, it was more about keeping them from poking around that building."

"Why, do you live there or something?" Could this be it? The elusive Orpheus lair? It looks so much like a normal apartment building, it's hard to imagine a vicious killer calling it home.

"You're smarter than this, Little Hood."

"Um, I'm sorry. What the hell did you just call me?"

A sly grin crosses his face. "Little Hood."

"Well, I don't like it." I cross my arms and lift my chin, causing my hood to slide back and reveal my kohl-lined eyes..

"Then tell me what you're really called."

I open my mouth but don't find the words. The truth is, I can't tell him my alter-ego name because I don't have one. Nothing ever fits right. Anytime I try to brainstorm, I just come back to my father's name. But Phantom Jr. or Phantom Woman sounds like a cheap copy of the real thing. Like I don't have my own identity.

Instead of answering, I size up the building and then the restaurant beside it. "The windows overlook the restaurant."

"Observant. Before I was so rudely interrupted by this guy, I was watching the Nightshade meeting."

I frown. "Why?"

"I patrol this part of the city." He gestures at the long stretch of street that disappears into darkness. "If something important happens here, it's my responsibility to know about it."

"Well, I need to talk to Layla Pirelli."

"You're not the only one."

"What does that mean?"

"If this chat is going to continue much longer, I suggest we go inside rather than stand here by a dead man." Orpheus slides his hands into his jacket pockets in a strangely familiar way and walks away from the body sprawled on the ground.

"Okay, you have a point." I glance up at the building's dark windows. "But how do I know you're not going to kill me with that gun in your pocket?"

"I refuse to dignify that with a response." He sets off at a brisk pace, leaving me alone with the vampire's blank eyes staring up at me. "If you want to chat, I'm going back inside. Otherwise, see you next time."

I stand rooted to the spot. Every inch of my body itches to follow, but my opinion of Orpheus still hasn't changed, even if he is my mate. Dad may have declared a truce with this vampire, but that doesn't mean I should. He murders people every single night. I don't want to give him the wrong idea. I don't accept what he does, and I certainly don't accept that he's my mate.

On the other hand, he's clearly up to something. And he knows more than he's letting on.

With a sharp shake of my head, I follow him into the building and up a flight of stairs. We enter a dingy apartment devoid of any life other than a red stain spreading across the carpet. I decide not to ask about that.

Orpheus waves me over to the window, and I peer down at the meeting exploding below. I try to ignore the heat of him beside me. The Boss and a heap of Soldiers stomp around arguing in a storm of testosterone. Layla Pirelli slumps in the middle of it all, mouth squeezed shut so tight her lips look like a raisin.

"What's going on?" I ask.

"That's the question," Orpheus says. "They don't seem very happy with her, do they?"

"Yes, but." I press my lips together. Orpheus doesn't know the details of my father's situation. Or does he? I glance sideways at him, but his blank—very chiseled, very handsome—face hides any insight into his thoughts. In any case, it makes no sense for Layla to be in trouble with the Boss. Didn't she agree to point the finger at Phantom for him?

I jiggle the window frame, but Orpheus snakes out a hand to stop me. "Better not. They might notice."

I glance down at where his hand clamps around mine. Even though we both wear gloves, heat pours into my skin, which catches me off guard. Heart pounding, I look back up at his face. His dark eyes are locked on mine. A strange need pulses in my chest. Every instinct inside of me begs for me to draw closer to him. He's my mate, and I—

I can't. Gritting my teeth, I pull away.

"Well, standing here is entirely pointless." I press an ear against the window, but it doesn't do any good. The glass muffles every shout of the argument. "I can't hear what they're saying."

"You really don't understand the concept of patience, do you?" He shifts in closer. Everything within me tightens at that.

I wonder what his chest feels like. The dips and ridges, the warmth of his skin. He looks strong enough to toss me over his shoulder, hold me against the wall, and...

My cheeks flame.

I back a few steps away from the window to put some distance between us, jumping when the floorboards creak. "No wonder you and Phantom get along. You sound just like him."

"Rude."

"Being like Phantom isn't an insult." I fold my arms and shoot him a glare. "He's the best fighter I've ever seen. And he doesn't have to kill to take anyone down."

"I'd argue he's never actually taken anyone down."

"You're infuriating."

"Mission accomplished, then." He pokes a long, gloved finger at the window. "Look, there's movement."

"Anything to stop this conversation." I turn back to the

window and elbow Orpheus out of the way. Outside, the Soldiers have returned to their seats and their untouched pizzas. The Boss backs away from Layla and grabs a glass of blood from the table, holding it out for someone to fill. With a muffled shout, the Mad Hatter tosses his hat into the air and clinks his glass with Bobby's.

Layla spins away from the party and hurries inside the restaurant with her head down. Time to make my move. But the second I turn toward the staircase, Orpheus clears his throat. My body freezes out of its own volition.

"Let me guess. You're going to confront Layla now."

I spin on my heels and fist my hands. "Is that a problem?"

"Half of the Nightshade gang is sitting in the back of her restaurant."

"They won't see me," I say. "They're too busy drinking blood to notice Layla leave."

"I really advise against this plan." His voice is as soft as a caress. He crosses the floor, vaguely reminding me of someone else, though I can't pinpoint who. Is this just the fated mate bond fucking with me?

"Of course you do," I say. "You just want to murder them all. Why talk when you can shoot?"

His eyes darken. Again, there's something strangely familiar in the way he looks at me. "It's dangerous, Little Hood."

"Why do you care?" My hand aches to reach up and brush the hair out of his face to get a closer look at him. These words, those eyes, it's all too familiar.

"Despite what you believe, I'm not all bad." He turns away from me and moves to the top of the stairs. "If you insist on doing this now, I'm coming with you."

"You know what?" I throw up my hands and follow. "Fine. Just don't shoot anyone."

We make our way back outside and past the long fence line. Laughter booms from the back of Four Points Pizzeria, a sound that scrapes against my eardrums. They don't have a right to be so happy, not when they make so many lives a living hell. At least the ice shower has stopped, though the storm clouds rolling overhead warn the sky isn't done with us yet.

"You seem cranky," he says as he follows me down the block.

"You have no idea." We pause when we reach the restaurant's windows. I roll onto my tiptoes and grit my teeth when my boots rub against the blister. Ignoring the pain, I look inside. Layla Pirelli heads to the front door, slamming a cigarette pack against her palm.

"Aren't you going to ask me why I want to talk to her?" I ask when we start moving again.

"No." He shrugs. "It's about the Saints believing Phantom murdered an angel. Don't look so surprised. I told you I make it my business to know what happens in this city."

We edge up to the side of the building, and I peer around the corner. A waiting crowd mills outside the front door, bundled up for winter. And just behind them, Layla leans against the brick wall, puffing at a cigarette with one hand and smashing her thumb on a phone with the other. As soon as the cell slips out of sight, I make my move. I'm down the block before Orpheus can blink.

"Hi," I say when we reach her. "I'm Phantom's friend. We need to talk."

She opens her mouth, but I press my gloved palm against her lips. "Don't even think about screaming for help."

"Little Hood, we're being watched." Orpheus nods toward the crowd, no longer milling around. They're all staring in our direction.

"Let them." I turn back to Layla. Her eyes are as wide as

dinner plates, the skin beneath them puffy and purple. She shivers in her knit sweater and reeks of stale cigarettes, but her hair is a smooth as a freshly-waxed motorbike. "I just have a few questions. Understand?"

She nods, and I drop the hand away from her mouth.

"What do you want to know?" she asks in a wobbling voice.

"I want you to tell the truth. Whatever they're giving you to lie to the Saints, I'll give you double." To show her I'm serious, I pull a small collection of vampire saliva vials from my pocket. "There's way more where this comes from."

"No." She whips her head back and forth between me and Orpheus. "It isn't like that."

Orpheus pulls the gun from his pocket and levels it at Layla's waist. She whimpers and stumbles away from us, pressing her back tight against the brick wall.

"For fuck's sake, Orpheus. What are you doing? This isn't part of the plan."

"*Your* plan. Mine is different." He steps closer to Layla and pokes her belly with the gun. "Did you actually witness Phantom murder an angel?"

"No!" A tear leaks out of her eye and slides down her cheek, leaving a streak of black mascara behind. "I swear. I wasn't even there. I was at home in bed. All I did was call the Saints and tell them what he told me to say."

"And Nicky Tanner was definitely an angel? Not a fae or a shifter or a vampire?"

I frown at Orpheus. That thing again?

"I don't know," Layla whispers.

"So, you admit you saw nothing." I move in front of Orpheus, my back pressing against his chest. "Orpheus, put the gun away. You're freaking her out."

Orpheus puts his gun in his pocket, but he keeps his hand

there, too. No doubt he'll rip it out again. He won't kill anyone on my watch, though. And especially not an innocent witch, cowering in a sewage puddle and gripping her cigarette pack as if it's a lifeline.

"Okay," I tell her. "Here's what's going to happen. You're going to go to the Saints tomorrow and tell them you lied."

"I swear I will." She pushes away from the wall and grabs my hand with trembling fingers. "I promise. First thing in the morning. I already told the Boss I would."

"What?" I frown. "Wasn't he the one who asked you lie to them?"

Her eyes well up with tears, and she glances at the restaurant. "I thought I was doing it for them, I really did."

"If it wasn't for them, then who the fuck was it for?" Orpheus asks from behind me.

"I can't tell you." She sniffs and scrubs at the mascara on her cheek with her sleeve. "I won't betray him."

The door of the restaurant flies open. Bobby Shade stomps out onto the sidewalk, flanked on both sides by the Mad Hatter and four of his Soldiers. Several patrons in the crowd gasp and back away. The others whip out their cell phones and aim it at the vampires and us, snapping pictures. *Great*.

"Layla," the Boss says with a heavy sigh when he spots us. "Honey, I warned you what would happen if you talked."

He flicks his fingers, and several vampires rush toward us, including a laughing Mad Hatter. Layla screams and bolts down the street. Orpheus and I exchange a look. In unison, we pivot and set off at a run. My arms pump at my sides, and my feet slam hard against the pavement. I grind my teeth at the pulsing blisters growing bigger with each passing beat.

I could spread my wings and fly, but I would struggle to make it through the narrow alleys. Plus, half the time they don't listen to me. And I need to get to Layla before the vampires do. Otherwise, they'll kill her.

Up ahead, Layla jumps over a broken crate discarded in the middle of the alley. Orpheus soars over it, and I follow. The jagged wood snags my leggings. A *rip*, and a sharp slice. Blood spurts from the wound, and I fist my hands to block out the pain. Behind me, the thunder of footsteps drifts away, though there's no way we could have outrun them already.

Layla runs into the middle of the next street. A car swerves up onto the sidewalk to avoid a crash. The driver emits a string of yelled profanity while blaring on the horn. Orpheus follows, me limp-running just behind. When Layla reaches the other side of the street, she darts into an alley.

My feet tangle up when they splash into a puddle, and I fall palm first onto the ground. Brilliant stars blind my eyes. Groaning, I roll onto my back and stare up at the sky. Orpheus drops back and looks down at me.

"Are you all right?" He actually looks concerned.

"Absolutely terrific." I start to push up from the ground and wince from the new additions to the bruise factory.

His nostrils flare, and then he kneels beside me. "You're hurt. I can smell your blood."

"What are you going to do? Bite me?"

"I don't drink blood that way." He holds out his hand. "But the Nightshade vampires definitely do."

Despite my every intention to ignore his hand, I slide my gloved fingers into his open palm. Tension pounds against my skull, and the blood loss—definitely the blood loss—causes my vision to swim. Slowly, Orpheus pulls me from the ground, and as if my feet are working against me, I stumble into him.

He catches my elbows, and I swallow hard. I'm pinned against his chest, and I can smell the leather, the musk, the steel.

My heart tumbles as I find myself looking up into his heated gaze.

And then a delirious thought pops into my mind. I want him to kiss me.

"Maybe we should let her go," he murmurs. "Get you home and bandaged up."

There's something in his voice that makes his words sound far more suggestive than they really are.

"No," I whisper back. "They're going to kill her."

"She's fast. They'd have to catch up."

"You have a point."

He still holds my elbows, and my palms move to his chest. Beneath my fingers, his muscles tense.

"There's something I need to tell you," he says.

In the distance, a shot rings out. Orpheus steps back, and my hands drop to my sides. Heat scorching my cheeks, I turn away. Without another word, we hurry down the alley toward the sound. We sidestep crates and sewage puddles and ignore the rotting stench rolling off an open dumpster. And mostly ignore each other.

When we spill out of the alley, I stumble to a stop with horror twisting my gut. Layla Pirelli sprawls across on the center white line, her dark hair spilling from her bun like a halo. Blood leaks from a hole in her forehead and drips into vacant eyes. Teeth marks mar her neck.

"Fuck." I clench my fists.

Footsteps echo through the empty street. I reach for Orpheus instinctively and turn toward the sound.

The Mad Hatter steps from the shadows. "The Boss requires an audience with you two."

CHAPTER 11
SILAS

I angle my body between Gwen and the Mad Hatter. "Let her go, and I'll come with you."

The vampire spits out a laugh, and he lifts a long-barreled pistol in the air for my inspection. "Not an option."

I pull my hands from my pockets and show him my own weapon. The barrel glistens beneath the street lamps. "You'll have to get through me first, and I'm not that easy to kill. Let her go."

Out of the corner of my eye, Gwen runs toward him. A strangled yell rips from my throat. What the hell does she think she's doing? The Mad Hatter's eyes flick to Gwen, giving me an opening. I level my aim at him. Before I can shoot, he points his gun at her, and my impeccable aim falters.

If he hurts her, I will destroy him.

"Don't you fucking dare." I storm forward, my finger pulsing on the trigger.

The Mad Hatter shifts his attention back to me, even as Gwen bears down on him. Any second now, he'll make his move and shoot. Whether it's me or Gwen, I don't know. All I know is I have to stop it from being her.

Gwen closes in and throws a running left hook at the Mad Hatter's face. *Good girl*. His hat goes flying, and a gunshot peppers the night. Narrowing my eyes, and I squeeze the trigger just as the Mad Hatter's neck snaps back. The shot I fire ricochets off a utility pole and lodges into the closest building.

For fuck's sake.

He growls and takes a swing at Gwen, who dips down and places her palms flat on the ground. She sweeps out a kick, but the Hatter dances back. She pops up with fists raised. He mimics her stance. Slowly, they spin around each other, step by careful step. I steel myself and make my aim, but if I miss, the bullet may hit Gwen instead.

I won't risk that.

Besides, she's doing a pretty damn good job herself, even with a wounded leg. And it's *mesmerizing* to watch her work. I underestimated her.

I lower the gun just as the Mad Hatter barrels at Gwen. She jogs back and ducks when he throws out a fist. When she pops back up, she lets out a battle cry and throws her leg up into the air, her boot-clad foot slamming right into the Hatter's head.

A loud *crack* echoes down the street, The Hatter falls to the ground with Gwen heaving over him. Stunned silence is all I can manage for a moment.

And then I move to her side, smiling. "You just knocked out the Mad Hatter."

"These boots may give me blisters, but they sure as hell do the job." When she faces me, a brilliant smile lights up her entire face. Eyes sparkling, she pumps a fist into the night air. *That's my mate.*

"You are fucking amazing. Has anyone ever told you that?" The words spill from my lips before I can stop them.

Her cheeks deepen with color. Clearing her throat, she glances away. "Yeah, I do okay, I guess."

"More than okay."

She glances back at me, and her eyes search mine. I am more than aware of the distance between us, or the lack thereof. She's so close that I could kiss her right now. And with the fire in her eyes, I'm more than a little tempted to give in to the pull of her. To the pull of our bond.

She is the only thing in this godforsaken city that drives away the shadows.

But then I remember myself. She's Gwen Kane. I'm Orpheus. We're working together, and we're somehow fated mates, but I know she hates me. This can never be a thing.

Forcing myself to look away from her, I crouch down and take the Mad Hatter's gun before shoving the barrel into his forehead. Time to clean up the trash.

"What are you doing?" Gwen lays a hand on my arm.

"What does it look like I'm doing?" I look up at where she stands silhouetted by the pale moonlight. "This is Albert Armone. The Mad Hatter. The vampire who writes songs about murder and blood rage. Taking him out will be a win."

"You don't have to kill him to do that." She holds out a hand for my gun. "We'll call the Saints, and they'll come get him."

"For what reason?" Slowly, I rise and hand over the Mad Hatter's pistol, though only because it's Gwen Kane asking. "Getting kicked in the head?"

"*Murder*." She rolls her eyes and squats down to slide the pistol back into the Mad Hatter's gloved hand. Any moment now, she'll figure out why this little plot of hers will only float like a balloon shot full of lead.

"And why would they take him in for murder?" I ask.

She sighs and points to Layla Pirelli's prone form. "Um, hello. The body over there?"

"She was a witch. They won't care."

"But he has a gun in his hand." She whirls on me, and the hood falls from her head. The long ponytail cascading down her back snags my attention just long enough for her to extract my own pistol from my hand.

I frown. "So?"

"Maybe I can convince them to care more about what's happening in this city, especially when they find out who he killed. Layla went to them with 'information' about my father. They won't be happy someone killed her, and they can put the Mad Hatter in their dungeon." She puts my gun into the waistband of her leggings next to a can of pepper spray.

"*Or* I could just shoot him." I hold out a palm. "The Saints don't give a fuck about anyone but themselves. Give me my gun back please."

"Bad idea," a voice says from behind us. We both whirl to face the new arrivals. At least ten Nightshade Soldiers have joined us on the block. If she had just let me shoot the Mad Hatter, we'd both be out of here by now. But she didn't. And we aren't. I may be a decent fighter, and Gwen obviously has some skill, but this would be suicidal, even for me.

"Time to run." I grab Gwen's hand before she can choose the hard way out. She grunts and rips her hand away, but she doesn't argue. Instead, she pounds the pavement by my side, dodging into an alley when I point the way. A couple of shots ring out behind us, but we've ducked into safety just in time.

As we run, the pounding of footsteps begins to fade until the city swallows the noise. We pass streets bustling with open takeaways and seedy nightclubs, and then streets with long stretches of heavy silence, thick shadows, and skittering rats. After several blocks blur by, Gwen and I slow to a steady walk. She takes a long gaze around us and frowns.

"Where are we?" She tugs her hood around her face.

"A few blocks south of the Coils." I shrug my hands into my pockets and try to sound nonchalant. But my mind is reeling. "You can fly on home now. We lost them."

"Trying to get rid of me?" She narrows her eyes and picks up the pace. "Where are you going?"

"I'm going to see a man about a dog." After tonight's catastrophe, it won't take long for Nightshade to make a move. I need to get that weapon and finish this.

"Stop talking in riddles."

"You'll just tell me how terrible I am."

Gwen slows as we round the corner, only a few steps away from the Coils. "Try me."

"Okay." I stop and stare up at the slums, at the yellowed, sagging buildings shaped like frowns. "The building behind the restaurant has a direct view of the Nightshade tables. With the right weapon and enough bullets, I could take them out. Quick and easy."

She stares at me for a long moment before rounding to face me. I don't miss that she's put her back to the slums. "What happened to you to make you like this?"

"Nothing." I glance away from those eyes that almost weaken my resolve. "This is just who I am."

"But there's no honor in killing dozens of unsuspecting people, even if they are vampires. *You're* a vampire."

I flinch, and my voice slices as hard as steel. "Who said anything about honor?"

"I do." She places a palm on my cheek and forces me to face her. Everything within me tenses at her touch, and all my sharpened edges fall away. "I know this sounds crazy, but I feel like deep down inside you're better than this. I *know* it. Somehow."

"That's what you don't get. It's not about me. It's about them." Gwen's fingers on my face are very distracting, but I don't pull them away. "Those *people* do horrible things. They manipulate, they stalk, they kill. They drink innocents dry. All those humans trapped inside the Coils? They force them into it. They won't let them leave. And they do it all for what? Just because they can. Tell me why those vampires deserve to live. Tell me why I shouldn't kill them all and liberate the humans from that place."

She sighs and yanks her hand off my face, as if I'm a rattlesnake coiled to attack. "There has to be another way. I'm not going to let you do this."

"Good luck with that." I sidestep Gwen and cross the street to the Coils. Even though she doesn't know *who* I really am, she knows *what* I am. A killer. And I will always be a killer. With every step, I expect her to give up on me and fall back, but the clomp of her heavy boots never falters.

"You won't convince me not to do this," I say when I reach the metal jaws of the entrance.

Bracing myself for another verbal attack, I turn toward her. But Gwen's eyes no longer focus on me. She stares up at the looming slums, at the jagged metal entrance, at the caged balconies cluttered with stale laundry. She gasps in short, shallow breaths and claws at her throat. Her eyes are so wild, it's as if she's somewhere else other than here.

"Whoa, calm down." I gently lift her chin and stare into her eyes, but it's like she can't even see me. "What's going on?"

Her breathing turns to sucking coughs. Her knees buckle. I snake out an arm and catch her fall before lowering her to the pavement. She shakes violently, and the terror in her eyes is like a knife to my heart.

"Look at me," I say, holding her face between my palms. I rest my forehead against hers and take long, slow breaths. In and out, as if I can steady her breathing just by steadying my own. "Gwen. Look at me. Deep breaths. I've got you."

"Silas?" she asks between hysterical gulps of air. "Silas Thorn."

Her eyes roll back into her head, and her body slumps in my arms.

CHAPTER 12

GWEN

I wake with a start. A sofa creaks beneath me. I launch onto my feet and bend my knees in fight-stance mode through a hurricane of rapid breaths. Eyes wide, I scan my surroundings. A minimalistic room with a low ceiling and thin windows overlooks the dark, swirling river. A cube of ice slips down my spine. Where the hell am I?

Spinning, my eyes fly past a small kitchen and to a wall plastered with hundreds of newspaper clippings, photographs, and post-it notes. I gasp and step closer, fingertips skimming the rough edges. The articles date all the way back to the early eighties when the vampire gangs first infiltrated the city. Black-and-white candid photos of known leaders form a long line down one side of the collage. And above it all, an intricately-detailed hierarchy chart shows each member and their position within the vampire network. Some have harsh red markings over their faces. The dead ones.

"Gwen." Orpheus—no, *Silas*—says from behind me.

Whirling, I clench my fists in front of me, even though there's zero point. If he wanted to hurt me, he would have, instead of bringing me here, wherever the fuck *here* is. He still looks like Orpheus, though, except he wears an eerily normal pair of gray sweatpants with a fitted black tee.

The sweatpants are...distracting. And not for the first time, I notice just how muscular he is, with the ridges of his abs poking through his shirt. He looks good enough to eat.

Focus!

"Silas Thorn. I should have known it was you."

"I thought maybe you did," he says, watching me carefully, like I'm a cat ready to pounce on a bug. "How's your leg?"

I glance down. Dried blood speckles my socks and torn leggings, and a white bandage wraps tight around my calf. That wooden crate really did a number on me, but now the sharp stabs have eased into a mild throb. All because Orpheus, the assassin, cleaned and bandaged my wound. Something in my chest warms.

"You fixed my leg?"

"I didn't want you to get blood on my couch."

I narrow my eyes. "How do you look like someone completely different?" Though, now that I know, the resemblance is there. His face is slightly altered, but his body...those muscles are definitely the same. No wonder he seemed so familiar.

"An amulet. It protects me from sunlight, though I don't really need that until I'm older. And it makes me look like someone else when I wear it. Makes things easier for my assassinations."

Assassinations.

"Where the hell are we?"

I squint out the window at the long stretch of water that glistens underneath a dull moon. It's still nighttime, though there's no telling how many hours have slipped by.

"Boat Basin," Silas says. "I have a house here. It's only a couple of blocks from where you passed out."

Oh, that's right. I passed out. It's been years since I've had a panic attack that bad. My mother's face flashed in my mind before the world went black. Ghostly white and painted with blood. I gulp back the bitter sting in the back of my throat and force my thoughts toward Silas.

"So, how exactly did we get here?" I ask.

Silas shifts on his bare feet and stares at me with glittering eyes. "I carried you."

He says it so casually.

My lips part. The vampire assassin I just witnessed dragging a dead body into the middle of the street wrapped his arms around me, picked me up, and carried me to his home. The entire Silas puzzle is now laid out before me, but it still doesn't make any sense. The mismatched pieces all jumble together like some kind of painting of abstract art. There are so many questions I want to ask, so many things I want to know about this Silas-Orpheus fusion, but when I finally speak, the wrong thing pops out of my mouth.

"I guess this means you didn't get that weapon and commit mass murder."

Silas narrows his eyes. "No problem, Gwen. You're very welcome. I'm so glad I didn't leave you in the middle of the street to fend for yourself."

"Is this when you call me delusional again?"

"I wasn't planning on it, but the thought's now crossing my mind."

I wave at the floor-to-ceiling dedication to the Nightshade gang. "I'm not the one who has a detailed hit list on his wall. There's even a few angels on here, Silas."

"Seems you have everything you need to turn me in." Silas

shoves past me and rips an actual list of names off the wall. The scribbles stretch down both the front and back of the lined paper. The name at the very top is none other than Bobby Shade, the vampire he wants to kill like a coward instead of meeting him head-on with his fists. "Here you are. See if the Saints care about this. Or call the Houses. See what they say about No Man's Land. Do your worst to me, Gwen."

I push the paper aside and sigh. "I'm not going to turn you in."

"Why not?" he asks, but then continues before I have a chance to answer. "You won't turn me in because you know it's not as black and white as you say it is. These vampires escape justice every single day because there's no one in Towton City to enforce it. The Houses don't care about us. We have to take care of it ourselves."

"I'm not going to agree with you. No matter what you say."

"Well, I'm not going to agree with you, either." He tacks the paper back on the wall. "So, it's a good thing we can go our separate ways now. Layla is dead, which means no witness for the Saints. They'll let your father go, and you'll have no need to stomp around in my streets insulting me anymore."

The image of Layla's vacant stare imprints on my mind. We're responsible for her death, but Silas doesn't seem to care. "Layla said Nightshade wasn't behind framing my father."

"It doesn't matter who's behind it. They failed." He snatches a red marker attached to the wall and marks out Layla's name. I want to reach out and scrub the red away, but the marker is permanent and those lines will never be gone. "Without a witness, they'll let him go."

"You seem happy she's dead."

"I'm not thrilled about it, but it does mean your father goes free. Isn't that what you wanted?" He moves to the sliding door where he flips open the lock with a *click*. "In the meantime, we'll make a truce. You take Uptown, I take Downtown. You'll never have to see me again."

Frowning, the red slashes over Layla's name catch my eyes again. "On one condition. You give me one good reason why you should kill all those vampires."

"I already have." He snatches my boots from the floor and crosses the room. When he drops them at my socked feet, he refuses to meet my eyes. "To rid Towton City of the gangs, once and for all."

"The Saints and the Blackthorns would still be here." I frown up at him as I shove my feet into my boots. "They'd probably even thank you for it, especially the Blackthorns. Without Nightshade, they'll have more power. Or maybe that's what you want."

Silas stills. "Of course I don't want that."

"So don't do it."

"This conversation is over."

"It's over if you agree to hold off on your plan." I push up from the couch and edge in closer. His dark eyes flick back and forth as if he's searching for something in mine. My entire body coils tight when he drags his long fingers across his lips. I hold my breath and wait, though for what I'm not sure.

"Fine, I'll hold off," he finally says.

"Good."

"Good." He steps back, eyes shuttering. "Then, we have a truce."

READY, set, *punch*.

My fist soars at the punching bag and slams into the plastic in a beautiful chaotic frenzy. Grunting, I yank my hand back and bash the bag again. And again. And again. The white gauze wrapped around my hands scrapes against my bruised knuckles, but the adrenaline pumping through my veins dampens the sting.

I bounce on my tiptoes, suck in a deep breath, and wipe away the beads of sweat already slipping down my face. Levelling my gaze, the black bag's swinging form morphs into the Mad Hatter's cackling face.

Punch.

The slums sent me crumbling to my knees. Again.

Punch.

Silas Thorn is Orpheus, and Orpheus is Silas Thorn.

Punch.

He's my mate. And he hates me.

Punch.

The witness may be dead, but none of this feels over.

Punch. Punch. Punch.

"What did that bag ever do to you?" Kole pokes his head around the training room's cracked door and holds up a water bottle that glistens with sweat as much as I do.

I swipe my forehead with the back of my hand. "Stop lurking in the doorway."

"Does this mean I can come in?" Kole takes careful steps onto the gym mats and lets the door slam shut behind him, the noise echoing around us. My bedroom, the living room, and the kitchen combined could fit inside the training room with space to spare. Thick blue mats line every inch of the floor. A pull-up rig squats in one corner while a weight station sprawls across another. The cardio area includes a treadmill, a rowing machine, and a stationary bike. But the best part is this punching bag, the white label faded and the plastic cracked.

"It means I want that water. And some food." I take the bottle from Kole and empty the cool water into my parched mouth before splashing a few drops on my steaming face. My stomach grumbles and I motion for Kole to follow me to the kitchen.

"Want some breakfast?" I ask as I pad around the kitchen island, push up onto my toes, and grab a cereal bowl from the cabinet.

"No, I'm good." Kole perches on a stool, his spindly legs sticking out like tree branches, and lays his hands flat on the granite countertop. "What happened last night? I heard you stomping around at four, but when I came down, you were passed out in your clothes."

The slashes over Layla's name bleed into my eyes. Frowning, I tip the cereal box and watch the honey oats cascade into the bowl before dousing them in almond milk. "It's been taken care of."

"That sounds ominous."

"Ominous. Perilous. Sinister. All words that accurately describe last night." I narrow my eyes and stab my cereal with my spoon.

"It happened again, didn't it?" Kole's voice is quiet. "A panic attack."

Oh, right. *That*. "Well, it was one of the many things that happened."

"Gwen." Kole reaches across the counter and grabs my hand. "This sounds really dangerous."

"That's because it is really dangerous." I give him a weak smile. "But this is what I've been training for."

"You could get hurt, even with your angel strength. You're still half-human, Gwen."

"This is something I have to do. Whether you understand it or not." Pulling my hand out of his, I grab my half-eaten bowl from the countertop and dump the remains in the trash. Suddenly, my stomach aches far too much to eat. These past few days feel like two hurried walls closing in on me, and it's all I can do not to scream.

The stool scrapes against the floor when Kole stands and moves in behind me. Wrapping me up in a hug, he buries his nose in my hair and sighs. "I'm sorry. I just want you to be safe, that's all. Yes, I want to get your father away from the Saints. He's pretty much my dad, too. But I don't want to do it like this, not at the expense of losing you."

"I know." I close my eyes and lean into his arms. "But I think it's over now."

The patter of hurried feet makes me twist away from Kole. Elliott rushes into the kitchen, her broad-shouldered brother just behind her. They've both been staying in the apartment downstairs

And then I notice Elliott's pale cheeks. "Everything okay?"

"I just had another threatening phone call." Elliott's hand grips her cell phone. "They said they know where I am."

Those closing-in walls charge at me like a raging bull. With Silas, Layla Pirelli, and the panic attacks clogging up my thoughts, I'd forgotten about the threats aimed at Elliott.

I glance at Kole, and then hold out my hand for her phone. "What's the number?"

"It's blocked." She grips the granite countertop and leans into it. "Who are these people? Why won't they leave me alone?"

"She handed out more fliers today," Eric tells me.

I give her a look. "I'll tell you who they are. They're vampires. And you're threatening to shut down their blood bank."

"Yeah, well. They can fuck off out of Towton City. Those humans shouldn't have to feed them unless they want to."

She's right. But she's also putting herself in a lot of danger by continuing her campaign. I open my mouth to tell her just that, but my phone buzzes from the countertop.

I grab it, hope ballooning in my chest. Maybe this is the news I've been waiting for.

"Hello, this is Gwen," I say.

"Gwen." A sigh. "This is Alaric, from the Saints."

I smile. I knew it. "You're releasing my father."

A long pause follows. "I'm afraid I have some bad news. The witness checked out. Unfortunately, that means we'll have to treat him just as we'd treat anyone else. And the payment for angel murder is execution. I'm sorry, Gwen."

CHAPTER 13
SILAS

I lean on the back of the chair and stare up at the Nightshade wall. Someone on this wall has been working with my mother, and someone on this wall threatened Ronan. It's the only reasonable explanation. Layla thought she was helping the Nightshade gang because the vampire who asked her to lie to the Saints must be a member. But who? All of these individual strands are somehow linked.

If only I hadn't given Gwen my word, I could wipe the streets clean of these vampires once and for all.

Tabby pads over to me and meows. Purring, she rubs her face against my leg, and I bend down to scratch behind her ears.

"What do you think, Tabby cat?" I ask. "What do I do?"

A banging erupts on my sliding door. "Silas!"

I glance at the time on my cell phone. It's not even eight yet. A bit early for Mrs. Casey to be caught in a mishap already. When I slide open the door, a blast of bitter air swoops into the boat with a flurry of snow. Mrs. Casey wraps a flowery scarf tight around her frizzing hair and trots inside before I have a chance to open my mouth.

"Is everything okay, Mrs. Casey," I ask as I close the door behind her.

She rubs reddened hands together and frowns. "You listen to the ham radios much these days?"

"The radios? No." I shift to block her view of my Nightshade wall. She's never seen it, and it's best it stays that way. I don't want to scare her. "Why?"

She hugs her cable-knit sweater tighter around her shoulders. "Oh, Silas. I don't know how to tell you this."

"Tell me what?"

"It's that mother of yours, you see." She clasps my arm and presses her fingertips into my skin. "There's chatter that she's back in town."

I still. "Back in town."

"I'm so sorry, Silas. After everything she's done to you."

My canines ache, and I take a step back from Mrs. Casey. I read her lips when she says my name, but I don't hear. The world is on mute. Even my vision goes dark in the corners.

Isolde Thorn is back in town. Gwen once asked me why I am the way I am, and she's why. My mother made me into a monster. And now she'll find a way to make this entire city bow beneath her heel.

IT'S BEEN an hour since I discovered my mother escaped the doomed fate she only brought upon herself. And it's been fifteen minutes since I abandoned my boat to head straight into the slums. The truce with Gwen is null and void. When I agreed to the terms, my mother was still out roaming No Man's Land.

Now that she's back, I need to take care of Nightshade or a war will break out between the vampire gangs again. So many innocents will die.

The wind bites my cheeks until I duck through the entrance to the slums. When I hurry past Ronan's shop, I glance inside, but the only things to see are knock-off amulets and a blanket of dust. A few barefoot boys patter by, lugging pails of water from the public tap while a white-haired man carries a bag of rice on his back just behind them.

They pay no attention to me.

As I pass the next few shops on Bright Street, it's more of the same. Empty, still, calm. It's odd, but it's also early yet. I hit the intersection and snake to the left. The bulging pipes above rain down sewer water, but my umbrella shields my face from the attack. I pass a few sleeping forms and a food stall hawking fish balls and crackling pork. When I finally reach the staircase, I snap my umbrella shut and step onto the grated concrete blocks.

Step after step, I climb until I reach the fourth level of the slums. Several tunnel-like streets snake out before me, each leading to a different wing. One tunnel leads to a series of one-room dilapidated apartments. Another leads to a strip of brothels and gambling dens. And my choice of tunnel leads to the one human in this hellhole with weapons. He hoards them for Nightshade, and for whatever reason, he's never fought back.

I reach a red door with a faded dragon painted around a peephole, the eyeball acting as the view. I pound my fist, and moments later, the door creaks open to reveal a grizzly stick of a man. His matted gray hair hits a chin hidden behind a bush of curly beard, and grease stains the wife-beater sagging on his bony shoulders. Now, I start to understand why he does whatever Nightshade asks. They keep him drugged.

His dilated pupils flick up and down before he clears his

throat. "Figured you'd come here one day, but never expected it to be at ass crack o'clock. Will you at least let me put on a clean shirt so I can die with dignity?"

"I'm not here to kill you." I cross my arms over my jacket. "You may have a weapon I need."

He glances down at his wrist, but his skin wears nothing but moles. "It's a little bit outside my normal working hours."

I narrow my eyes and reach for my gun.

"Okay, okay." He creaks the door open wider and motions me inside. "I guess I can make an exception for you."

I step inside his home. Fetid air clogs my nostrils, a combination of unwashed bodies and room temperature meat. Yellowed mattresses pile up in the corner while rows of tables engulf the rest. Glinting weapons cover every surface.

"What're you looking for?" the man asks, scratching his beard.

"A semi-automatic sniper rifle with vampire bullets." I nod to the table holding the weapon I seek. "And a silencer."

The man lets out a low whistle and lifts one of the bigger rifles from the table. It's thin and and sleek with a barrel as long as my arm. "Now, I'm not sure if Nightshade would want me to give this to you."

"It's not their decision. It's mine."

He shrugs, and then packs the rifle, the silencer, and a decent supply of vampire bullets into a hard black case. When he hands it over, I lift my smaller gun from my pocket and point it at his head. "We're going to come to an agreement, or I'll shoot you right now."

He blinks and presses damp palms onto his baggy jeans. "Right, an agreement."

"If Isolde Thorn, or any of her people, visit you, you will take this orange cloth I'm going to leave you, and you're going to tack it up on the Bright Street intersection."

"Isolde? But she's gone."

I drive the barrel into his skull. "Not anymore."

"Okay, I'll do it." He licks his lips.

"Good." I fish the orange cloth from my pocket and shove it into his shaking hands. "I was never here."

I turn to go, but then I pause. "Maybe use these weapons for something good and get yourself and the others out of here."

But he won't. I know it, and he knows it. They'd have to leave the city, and it's as dangerous out there as it is in here, and none of the Houses would take them in. They're trapped here, with or without these weapons.

And they have nowhere else to go.

I LEFT the building behind the Four Points Pizzeria unlocked last night, and the front door swings open when I press it with my gloved thumb. With my senses on high alert, I climb the stairs and enter the third floor apartment I found last night. A suffocating silence descends when I step inside. Dust swirls into my eyes. The dark stain from the Soldier's death is the only evidence anyone has been inside this place for years.

I place the black case on the floor and begin unpacking. The human threw in a stand for good measure, and as I screw the pieces together, it's as if my future is building before me. All sharp glints and sleek vengeance. However I have gotten to this day, there is no turning back now. Wrongs will be turned right, and the city's stained streets will be wiped clean.

My mother will eventually get her claws into the Coils again, but at least there won't be a war.

I spend the next several hours practicing my aim, frowning at the falling snow, and preparing the room. While inside the slums, I traded for some heavy-duty bolts that I add to the apartment's door using a battery-powered screwdriver. Once the bolts are firmly in place, I move over to the fire escape window and fasten a cheap security grill. No Nightshade member can easily get inside this room within the next twelve hours, and that's all the time I need.

As a final touch, I toss a white sheet over the rifle and put on my amulet so that I look like Silas Thorn instead of Orpheus. I'll be back as soon as the sun dips out of sight, but first, there are a few more issues to deal with. I shut the building's front door behind me just as my cell phone buzzes in my pocket.

I glance at the screen. It's from Gwen Kane.

The Saints have decided to execute my father.

I suck in a breath. Gwen's fiery face flashes in my mind, her eyes red and full of bitter tears. *My mate.*

My tightened fist nearly shatters my phone. How can I stand aside and let this happen? The answer is, there is no how. The answer is, I can't.

My mind rages against me as I stand outside in the bitter cold. Helping Phantom means destroying myself. If I go to the Saints, they'll execute me instead of him, even if I tell them the Nicky Tanner I killed was a vampire. The city needs me, more than it needs Phantom.

But it's Gwen Kane, my mind whispers.

My eyes trail across the apartment building that holds the resolution to my vengeance, and then back to the cloud of snow leading to the Uptown streets. My vengeance will have to wait until another day. Perhaps until another life. Gwen can't wait. She needs my help now.

It's time I turned myself in.

CHAPTER 14
GWEN

I shove open the cathedral doors and storm inside. My boots click against the marble floor, echoing through the vast space. I ignore the glossy-haired angel who tries to greet me and head straight into the main room where Alaric lounges on a bench, staring up at the empty dais. In his all-black ensemble, he reminds me a lot of the other gang members who prowl the streets.

At the end of the day, the Saints aren't any different than Nightshade. Deep down, I'd always known that, but I'd wanted them to be above it all. Better than the rest of this city.

"I need to talk to you." I round the bench and stand before him, forcing him to look at me.

"Gwen." He sighs. "My phone call was not an invitation for you to come by."

"You cannot execute my father without evidence."

"We have evidence. That's enough."

"He didn't do it." I release my tight grip on my wings and allow them to spread behind me for the first time in months. To remind him we are the same. If he won't care about anyone other than angels, then so be it.

My back aches from the added weight, but the cool air of the cathedral is a soft caress across my pale feathers. I rarely ever fly. I find it harder than most angels because of the human blood running through my veins. But this does the job. It snags Alaric's attention.

"There was a rumor you couldn't spread your wings," he says with arched brows. "Glad to see your angel blood won over the human part of you."

He says it like it's an insult.

"I talked to Layla last night," I say, choosing to ignore him. "She says she lied to you, thinking it would help Nightshade. And it makes sense. They'd love to have Phantom off the streets."

Alaric frowns and glances away. "Yes, I heard about your trip to Four Points last night. You and Orpheus. It's interesting that she shows up dead after she accuses your father of murdering an angel. One might think you had Orpheus assassinate her. Then, we wouldn't have a witness, right? And Damian Kane could roam free."

I pull back, sucking in a breath. "You can't believe that."

"She was seen arguing twice last night." Alaric gives me a flat stare. "Once with her boyfriend, Vincent Shade. Once with you and Orpheus. Which one do you think is more likely to have lead to her death?"

"Neither. It was the Mad Hatter," I tell him. "I practically saw him do it."

"I'm afraid your word means nothing to me, Gwen." Alaric stands and wraps a firm hand around my arm, steering me toward the cathedral's lobby. "It's time for you to go. And don't come back again. You aren't welcome here."

"Wait." I try to jerk away from him, but it's no use. He's far too strong, and all my wings do is trail helplessly behind me. "Let me see my father."

"You can see him on his execution day, along with the rest of the city."

When I gape up at him, he just smiles.

"His public execution is in two weeks' time. To remind everyone that you cannot touch an angel without repercussions."

My heart pounds so hard I can barely breathe. "You can't do that."

"We're Houseless." He tosses me into the lobby. "We can do whatever the hell we want."

He grabs the doors of the main room and slams them into my face. The sound reverberates in my eardrums, drowning out the frantic beating of my heart. My eyes burn with tears as a hopeless chasm yawns wide before me. They're going to kill my father, for no fucking reason, and there's nothing I can do to stop it.

"We're Houseless," I whisper.

But that doesn't mean we have to stay that way.

Pacing the lobby, I pull out my phone and dial a number I've never used. One my father found a few months ago. Someone to call in case of an extreme emergency. And if this isn't an emergency, then I don't know what is. The line rings and rings and rings, and I start to think she'll see my number and refuse to answer. But then.

"Hi, this is Dannika." Her voice has a calming tone to it, but I can hear a hint of suspicion.

I close my eyes and sag onto the nearest bench. "Dannika. This is Gwen Kane. From Towton City."

A pause. "That city in No Man's Land."

"That's right," I say. "I...well, I think we need your help."

Quickly, I fill the half-shifter, half-vampire in on what's been happening here. According to my father, she's in a relationship with the King of the House Blood and Beryl, and she's a lot more open to helping Houseless supernaturals than most. The problem, of course, is that she's on the other end of the country, and even then it's a lot to ask. Houses don't run to the aid of a city in No Man's Land.

Earth and Emerald, the nearest House, never has.

"The Saints sound like assholes," she says when I finish telling my story.

"Accurate."

She sighs. "Right. Here's my advice. You should join Earth and Emerald. They're the closest House to where you are, and they're good for independent supernaturals like you. Just stay away from Fire and Fluorite. It's in shambles right now."

"I wasn't really planning on joining a House."

"You need to, Gwen. Trust me. Call up Earth and Emerald. Tell them what's going on and that you want to join. You'll be better off outside of No Man's Land."

I grip my phone tighter. This conversation has not gone as I hoped. I know Dannika is only trying to help, but her advice won't work for me. I'm not joining a House and leaving everyone else in this city to fend for themselves. It's all of us or none of us. And I know which one they'll choose.

They've never helped us in the past.

I end the call with Dannika after thanking her for the help, and push out into the cold with my wings flared behind me, running smack dab into Silas's muscular chest. He takes ahold of my arms as I stumble away from him. He's wearing his amulet, which means he looks like the guy I've spoken to at the pub a hundred times. But his eyes, so dark, so violent, they're Orpheus. The way they cut through me makes my breath catch, and it takes me a moment to remember that I haven't asked him to meet me here.

We parted on such bad terms.

"Silas?" I gaze up at him, my heart pounding with a frantic kind of energy. "What are you doing here?"

The truth is, I'm glad to see him. Silas Thorn—*Orpheus*—may be the only person in this twisted world who *will* fight, enough to save my father's life.

He glances up at the cathedral behind me. Has he come here to talk to Alaric, too? After my text, maybe he thought he could help. A wave of appreciation rushes through me.

"I need to talk to the Saints about something important." A muscle in his jaw ticks.

"Don't bother," I say with a harsh laugh. "I already tried. They think we killed Layla to keep her quiet."

His gaze snaps toward me. "What?"

I nod. "Listen, I'm sorry for how I reacted earlier. I'm just not used to your...methods. But I know you're only trying to do the right thing by this city."

"Gwen," he starts, clearly about to argue with me, but I beat him to the punch. I won't give him a chance to say no.

"We need to work together, Silas or Orpheus or whatever you want to be called. You were right. No one is coming to help us. We have to save this city ourselves," I say. "And now, it's time for war."

His eyes spark with an emotion I can't quite name, and he steps in so close that I feel the heat of him pressing against me. "Say that again."

"It's time for war," I whisper.

Orpheus drags a thumb across my lip, practically purring. "Careful what you say to me, Gwen. You're starting to sound like my mate."

CHAPTER 15
SILAS

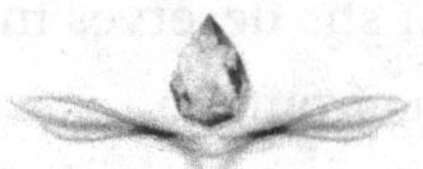

I'm fucked. Gwen shouldn't be here, not now, speaking of war and vengeance in a way that makes her eyes spark with fire. It makes me think of all the things I want to do to her, all the things I wish could vanish between us until it's just me and her. Nothing else.

"Your mate," she whispers, turning away. "I thought we weren't talking about that whole thing."

"Is that what you really want? To keep pretending like it doesn't exist?"

"Don't you?" She glances back up at me, and the look in her eyes is devastating. There's no hatred anymore. If we were two different people in a different world, maybe just maybe…

But no.

I came here for a reason. My life is over now, even if she's looking at me in a way that makes me want to taste her skin. If anything, it makes me even more determined. I need to save her father.

"Gwen," I say. "There's something you should know."

"No, there's something *you* should know."

"Gwen."

"Silas, *please*."

Inwardly, I groan. I can't say no to her, and the least I can do is hear her out. Then, I'll tell her—face to face—that I killed the supernatural named Nicky Tanner. Maybe she'll hate me forever, but she needs to know the truth. I could let her hear it secondhand from the Saints, but she deserves more than that from me.

She deserves *everything* from me.

"What do you want to tell me?" I shrug my hands into my pockets, to keep myself from touching her again.

She sighs, and her beautiful, brilliant wings vanish from sight. "You were right about Nightshade. We need to do something to stop them."

I frown up at the looming cathedral doors. The sooner this is over over, the sooner we can both move on. Her to a better life, and me to my fate. "You don't know what you're saying. This morning, you—"

"Forget about what I said this morning." She tugs on my arm and forces me to meet her eyes. "I know we have our differences, but don't you think we want the same things at the core of it? A better city. Safer streets. A life without the gangs. We can fight against all of this."

"What are you saying?"

She smiles, but this time, the expression doesn't quite reach her eyes. It's harsher than it usually is. This city is getting to her, too. "I'm saying I want to take down the vampire gang, starting with Vincent Shade."

"Wait. Vincent Shade?" I fall silent when a bundled shifter passes by us. As soon as he's out of earshot, I continue. "What does he have to do with this?"

"I'll explain everything to you if you come with me. And

when we win, we can take care of everyone trapped in the Coils. They won't be forced to feed vampires anymore."

My jaw tenses, and I shake my head. "You didn't hear, then."

"Hear what?"

"My mother is back in town. Even if we take down Nightshade, she'll still be here. She'll seize control of all the humans in this city, and she'll take over the Blood Market, too. She'll own it all."

Gwen blows out a breath. "Even more of a reason for us to join forces. I can't do this alone."

She looks up at me with fire in her eyes. *Fuck*. I can't turn myself in now. If I do, the gangs win. Gwen might get her father back, but it would be a short-lived victory. She seems to believe she has a way to save him, as well as take down the monsters of this city. It's impossible to say no to that.

"I'll come hear your plan, but I'm not making any promises," I finally say.

"Good." Gwen smiles, a real one this time. "You won't regret it."

She jogs down the remaining steps, her boots crunching the snow. When she points to her motorcycle, now covered by a thin film of ice, I can't help but laugh.

"Not that thing again. You drive like a maniac."

"You scared?"

"Don't flatter yourself." I climb on and shift back to make room for her. "Where are we going exactly?"

She doesn't answer as she hops on and starts the engine. I hold onto her waist. She cranks the engine and angles the motorcycle away from the curb, spinning us through the streets. Ice seeps through my jeans, and my jacket billows out behind me in the whipping wind.

After we pass several blocks, I slide my hands along the curve of her waist. I can't fucking help myself. Even though she's small and toned, her shape is like an hourglass, all curves and soft skin.

Gwen shivers against me, and I can't tell if it's from the freezing air or from my touch. But then she drops a hand to mine and curls her fingers against me, almost encouraging more.

I shift closer until her ass presses against me. My cock hardens with need. She feels so good with her body tucked up against mine. We fit together like puzzle pieces, and suddenly, I'm overwhelmed by the temptation to pull this bike over and carry her all the way back to my bed.

Her fingernails dig into me as she rocks back, lifting her ass a little so that it rubs against my cock. *Good fucking god.* I nearly groan out loud.

What I would give to taste her. What I would give to bury myself inside of her. I bet she's delicious. Even my canines ache from the thought of it.

She rocks against me once more, and then shudders.

I can't hold back anymore. I dip my face to her neck and lower my mouth. My canines skim along her delicate skin. She leans into me, tilting her head in invitation. Tension pounding through me, I kiss the spot between her neck and shoulder. The sweet scent of coconut floods my senses.

She trembles. I drag my tongue up the side of her neck and tease the delicate skin below her ear. Her hand tightening against mine, she drags my fingers around to her front waistband and then leans back against me.

A purr builds in my throat. Are we doing this? Does my *mate* want me to pleasure her the way I know that only I can?

I slide my hands between her thighs, annoyed by the thick material in the way. Still, the heat of her pushes against me. I rub her core and kiss her neck and—

The motorcycle jerks to a stop.

Sucking in a breath, I ease back, my cock throbbing with need.

Gwen pulls off her helmet and whispers, "We're here."

She doesn't look at me. She doesn't say anything about what just happened. She just stares up at the formidable-looking building with flushed cheeks and bright, bright eyes.

"Put your hands back on the handlebars. I'll finish what I started, darling."

Her flush deepens. "I got carried away. We should go inside."

"Suit yourself." I smirk when she brushes her hair back from her face and straightens her jacket. She can pretend all she wants, but I see the need in her eyes. Hell, I felt it with my fingers.

"What's that?" she asks, pointing down the street.

I follow the line of her finger. Several black cars lurk at the curb. There are figures inside, but their faces are hidden by the tinted windows. The rumble of their engines drifts toward us.

"Nightshade. Or Blackthorn. It's hard to say."

Her face pales. "How did they find my house? We keep our identities secret."

"Not secret enough."

Gwen scowls and punches a number into the dashboard keypad. The garage door rolls up in front of us. With a loud crank of the engine, she drives the motorcycle into a parking spot and closes the door behind us.

"You have a good set-up here. I doubt they can get inside," I say.

She climbs off the motorcycle and frowns. "But now they'll know every time I leave. They might even follow us. That's going to make things difficult."

"On the plus side," I say as I ease off the bike, "you don't have to worry about an alter-ego name anymore. Unless you have one and just didn't want to tell me."

She walks over to an elevator door and stabs the up button. "No, I don't have one. I thought I had more time to decide."

"Really? I pegged you as picking a name in the womb." I stride into the elevator behind her and pull off my jacket. A dusting of snow sprinkles the metallic floor.

Gwen frowns as we slide up past the second story. "When I was in the womb, my mom was still alive. She's the entire reason I do this. So no, I didn't pick one out then, did I?"

Ah.

"I'm sorry," I say, wanting to wrap my arms around her to wipe that dark look off her face. "I didn't mean to bring it up."

The elevator door slides open to reveal a third floor just as sleek and starkly-decorated as my own boat. Black furniture, white walls. No color at all. We step into the entryway, and Gwen hangs up our jackets before motioning me to follow her into a living room with massive windows overlooking the city. She settles onto a leather couch and glares at the television screen as if it's responsible for everything wrong in her life, when she should really be glaring at me.

I join her on the couch and choose my words carefully. "Phantom told me you were there when it happened."

"Yeah, he told me that, too," she says with a sigh.

"You mean you don't know?"

"I mean I don't remember." She points at her forehead. "Whatever happened isn't in here anymore, and if you don't mind, I'd like to keep it that way."

"Talking about it might help the panic attacks."

She narrows her eyes. "Or we could talk about you instead. Why do you hate your family so much?"

"Besides the obvious?" I let out a bitter laugh.

"There has to be more to the story."

There's a reason I live on a fairly secluded boat far away from the majority of Towton City residents. I have my own life, and I don't share it with anyone. Ronan and Mrs. Casey both know my history, yet they never heard it from me. It's not something I like to talk about.

But things with Gwen are different somehow. Her eyes make me come undone.

"She abandoned me in the Coils when I was eight." My tongue feels heavy and dry when I speak the words, but I keep going. "For an entire year. She just left me there to rot."

Gwen's mouth drops open, and she shifts closer. "That's why…"

"That's why I love the slums." And somehow, saying it aloud hasn't caused the ceiling to drop on top of me or the floor to swallow me whole. The Coils were more a home to me than anywhere else in my life, even more than my boat. Maybe that makes me part of the darkness, but maybe that's not such a terrible thing.

"What happened?" Gwen asks. "How did you survive? Your fangs wouldn't have dropped by then."

"A kind human man named Ronan found me squatting in the sewage. He took me in, and I lived with him until my mother came back a year later to fetch me. I didn't want to go with her, but…I thought I had to."

"But…*why*? Why did she do that?"

"Why?" I shrug my shoulders, the answer to all questions relating to my mother. There is no real *why*. "She's a sociopath."

"I don't understand."

"She is just a goddamn sociopath. She didn't want me around for awhile so that was that. Humans mean very little to her, and neither did I. So, she threw me in there with them."

Gwen's face falls. This is why I never tell anyone about my past. I don't want pity. A lot of people go through shitty childhoods, and then blame their shitty actions on it. My past doesn't excuse anything I've done, including but not limited to sitting here and letting Gwen think I had nothing to do with her father's fate.

"Don't give me pity, Gwen," I say. "I was better off in the slums with Ronan. I'm not a Blackthorn. Not really."

"Gwen?" Kole Mason pokes his head into the living room and glances at me. From his lack of surprise, it's obvious he's been listening to our conversation. For how long, who knows. "I have something I really need to tell you, but…it's private."

"Private how?" She shoves up from the couch with a glint in her eye.

"It has to do with your father and his office." He ducks his head to step inside the living room, never taking his eyes off me.

"Go ahead. Silas is part of the team now."

"There's a team?" I ask with a frown. "I wasn't aware there was a team."

"Stop complaining. Kole's been trying to figure out a way into Dad's office."

"Good luck with that. He told me once that his office is rigged with explosives, just in case someone tries to break in."

"Except I've been coming up with possible combinations for the lock, not trying to break in." Kole clears his throat and shifts Gwen sideways as if that's going to prevent me from hearing his words. "Gwen, I'm sorry, I have to ask. Why is Silas Thorn here?"

"He's here because he's Orpheus, and he's going to help," she says. "So, did you find a code that works?"

"I'm sorry. What? Silas Thorn is Orpheus?" Kole swivels his head and stares as if he's seeing me for the first time. And in truth, he is. Silas Thorn isn't my real self. As if to prove it, I take off my amulet and drop it onto the coffee table, revealing my true form.

Kole's jaw drops.

Gwen pushes up onto her tiptoes and snaps her fingers in front of Kole's eyes. "Hey. We can go into that later. Code news. Now."

"Right." Kole drags his eyes away and hands Gwen a scrap of notebook paper. "Well, I haven't tried it yet, but what do you think of this?"

"Of course," she says in a whisper.

CHAPTER 16
GWEN

Kole is a genius. Why haven't I thought of this before? His familiar scribble covers the lined paper with dozens of number combinations that mean something to both me and my father. Birthdays, anniversaries…deaths.

But one scribble at the very bottom stands out from the rest. It's a transcript of that conversation I had with my father when I first found out the Saints locked him up. His words didn't make any sense at the time, which is why I recited them to Kole in the first place, and now it's obvious why. The conversation was a code.

There are four *things I need to tell you.* One *is that the Saints have decided to keep me for awhile.* Two, *you need to stay out of this. Don't do anything stupid. You aren't* nine *anymore. You need to be responsible.* Four, *go to your job today and don't miss any of your* seven *working hours.*

Four, one, two, nine, four, seven. It's a six-digit code.

"My shifts at the pub are never seven hours," I say. "And there isn't a third thing. He skipped right to four."

"Will someone please explain what's going on?" Orpheus—Silas—stands from the couch and moves in behind me to peer over my shoulder at the paper. His arm brushes against my back, and shivers rake through me. He's taken off his amulet, and that harder, rougher version of him is back.

Admittedly, I like him best this way.

I try not to think about that moment on the motorbike. Honestly, I don't know what got into me. It was as if my body just took over, full of heat and a strange, dark need for that rock hard length Silas pressed against me. And his hand between my thighs. If I'd kept driving for a little longer, I'm not sure what would have happened.

What's worse is, a part of me definitely wants to find out.

I swallow. "My father called me the morning after the Saints took him. He said this to me."

"A bit wordy for Phantom." Silas's breath hits the back of my neck, right where he kissed me, sending a rocket of warmth across my cheeks.

I really need to get a grip.

"He was trying to give you the code to his office," Kole says.

"Possible." Silas nods. "Maybe he'll have something in there that can help us take down the gangs."

Koles eyes widen. "What are you talking about?"

Quickly, I fill Kole in on what happened. I still haven't shared the Vincent Shade information with Silas either, and I explain what Alaric told me. Vincent Shade was Layla's boyfriend, and they got into an argument that same night.

"So, you think Vincent is involved," Silas says after several moments of silence.

"Layla said she thought she was helping the Nightshade gang by lying to the Saints. And then she refused to betray whoever it was. Makes sense it's her boyfriend. Maybe he's even the one who killed the angel. He could be behind the whole thing."

Silas shifts on his feet with an uneasy glint in his eye. "Unless we get proof, the Saints won't believe it."

"True," I say frowning at him. "So, we need to come up with a plan. Any ideas?"

"Well, I do have an idea. But you won't like it."

"Let me guess. You want to kill them all."

He surprises me by saying, "No. That won't get your father away from the Saints. We need to get Vincent Shade to confess to setting him up."

"You know what I think?" Kole asks with a hand raised in the air. "We should do all this planning stuff in the office, using the code *I figured out*."

"You're right," I say. "There has to be something useful in that office." Like a note from my father explaining exactly what steps I should take to get him out of the cathedral dungeon? That would be nice.

Kole leads the way to the elevator, and we all cram inside. He pushes the button for the basement, something I've done at least a thousand times, but I've never gotten further than that. When the elevator slides to a halt, Kole punches the numbers into the security keypad, and we all hold a collective breath.

The security light flashes green, and the doors whisk open before us. We wander into the room, and I spin to take it all in. My father has gutted one side of the building so that his office comprises of two floors. The ceiling looms far above, and on every side, shelves and shelves of books, vials of vampire saliva, bundles of fae hair, and collections of angel feathers line the oak walls. Overhead, a catwalk spreads out in four directions with ropes and chains dangling from the ceiling.

"Look at that," Kole says in a hushed voice that echoes up to the catwalk. "You have enough goods here to last a lifetime."

He wanders over to the massive computer squatting in the very center of the large room. Four monitors sit atop a curved black desk, all silent and still other than the occasional whir. He settles into the black swivel chair and hunches over to poke at the buttons. The screens fill with maps and a jumble of symbols and words that might as well be a foreign language to me.

Turning, I drag my eyes across the hundreds of book titles. Everything from history to gardening to magical stones. All of those neverending hours my father spent in here, I thought he'd been designing plots to take down the gangs. And maybe he did that sometimes. But now I see there's more to it than that. Creases dent the spines. These books are not untouched.

A flash of pink catches my eye. An entire floor-to-ceiling shelf holds my mom's old books in a carefully organized color grid, just like the way she used to do it. Pink and red romance novels sit next to blue-spined chick lit about country girls making their way in the big city. My eyes flood with tears, but I blink them back before any can spill onto my cheeks.

No crying, Gwen.

Not today.

Silas comes up beside me and eyes the bookshelf with a gentle smile. "This is an interesting collection for Phantom. I didn't know he had a secret love for romance novels."

"They were my mom's books," I manage to whisper. "I didn't know he kept them."

I pull a book from the shelf and glance down at the cover. A half-naked man and woman curl together on a silk sheet. Silas smirks, and heat floods my body, just as it did on the motorcycle. When his fingers slipped between my thighs. When his lips caressed my skin. Quickly, I flip open the cover, and my mom's looping handwriting jumps up at me.

Property of Olivia Kane.

My hands twitch, and the book plummets to the floor. When it hits the hardwood, the *thump* echoes over and over and over again. I press a hand against my heart to steady my breath while Silas lifts the book from the ground. He carefully slides it back onto the shelf, drops a warm hand on my shoulder, and squeezes. I look up and meet his eyes. He's so close. If I moved an inch, my nose would brush against his.

I could feel his lips on me again. The heat of his touch. The whisper of his canines. A sudden thought pops into my head before I can stop it. I wonder what it would feel like for him to taste my blood.

He's my mate.

"Everything okay?" Kole's booming voice makes my bones jump.

"Yeah, fine." I twist away from Silas and move over to where Kole perches in the computer chair and clicks around on the keyboard. My heart is beating so hard that I'm certain Silas can hear it, but I pretend like everything is normal.

Everything is completely normal. I'm not daydreaming about you digging your fangs into my neck and drinking me while slipping your hand down my pants and—

I cough. Too loud to be natural.

"Find anything?" I ask in a tight voice.

"Well," Kole says. "Did you know he used to own the building where they have the Blood Market? He still has access to the cameras there."

Silas peers over Kole's shoulder. "You've figured all this out already? I think I underestimated you."

"I'm going to take that as a compliment, even though it

doesn't sound like one." Kole exes out of a spreadsheet and clicks on a desktop icon. "But yeah, these programs are pretty straightforward."

"Kole's the brains. I'm the brawn."

The glint in Silas's eyes when he looks my way rattles me to my core. He smiles and glances down at my waist, and a hint of his sharp canines pokes through. Before I know what I'm doing, I round the chair to put some distance between us, like he might bite me right here in front of Kole.

He probably wasn't even looking at my waist anyway, and so what if he was? It's just a waist. Of course, he was practically caressing it on the bike. While kissing my neck. And pushing his cock against my ass.

Kole's voice zaps me back to reality. "This program is kind of creepy. You can search for someone, and look what happens."

Kole types in the name *Vincent Shade*, and long list of information scrolls down the screen. Some of these details must be well-known, but other bits are clearly information my dad has gathered over the years. The file includes his name, age, address, and his status as a known Soldier of Nightshade, along with a list of suspected but not proven murders. There are lots of photos of him.

But what catches my eye the most is a link to a phone tap. I don't know when, and I don't know how, but at some point, my father tapped the Nightshade phones.

Silas lets out a low whistle. "Phantom does not joke around."

"It's like your hit list wall on steroids," I say.

"Maybe we can use this information against Vincent?" Kole asks before closing out the file and typing another name into the search bar: Isolde Thorn. When the results scroll out, I shake my head and frown. There's barely anything here. Her age and address fields are blank, and there are no photos. And definitely no phone tap.

"Don't look so surprised," Silas says. "She leaves no trace. I doubt Isolde is even her real name. Though I did think Phantom would have more on her than this."

"But you have her last known address, right?" I ask.

"Not a chance."

"A phone number?"

Silas shakes his head. "She doesn't trust me with her contact information. You know just as much as I do."

"So, question," Kole says, spinning in the computer chair to face us. "What's the plan?"

"I have an idea." Silas turns to me. "Gwen, you're going to contact Vincent. You'll tell him to meet you in the building behind Four Points Pizzeria and that under no circumstance is he to tell anyone about it."

"Sounds good to me."

"Wait." Silas chuckles. "You might not like the rest."

I arch a brow. "Why not?"

"Think about it. Doesn't it seem like a coincidence that my mother shows up in town right after Phantom gets framed for murder? She's involved in this, and if we're going to take Vincent down, she's going down with him."

"Good point," I say with a slow nod.

"Kole can stay here and listen to Vincent's wiretap, just in case he decides to contact my mother and tell her you called. Gwen, you'll wait outside Vincent's house and follow him. If he goes to see her first, we'll know."

"Right. I can see now why you thought I wouldn't like this."

"We need ears." He points at Kole, and then he points at me. "And we need eyes. We also need someone who's willing to follow through on a threat. I'll be the one who talks to Vincent if he shows."

I open my mouth to argue, but he cuts me off.

"No, I won't kill him, but that's not the point. The point is that I'm willing to, and everyone knows it. We need to get him talking so that he admits to framing Phantom. My Orpheus reputation might make all the difference in the world."

"Fine." I nod. "And this time, record whatever the asshole says. If the Saints want proof, let's give them proof."

"There's just one potential problem," Silas says with a grim smile. "We need to get out of this building without anyone seeing us, and we have a bunch of Nightshades or Blackthorns watching that door."

Kole whirls around and pokes at the keyboard. "I think I've got that one covered."

CHAPTER 17
SILAS

Kole swivels to the second monitor while gnawing at a pencil stuck between his teeth. He twists his long legs underneath him and pokes at the keyboard, forehead furrowed like a pug. A moment later, the screen brightens, displaying a blue and white document of a four-story building.

"This was already up on the screen when we walked in." He taps at the monitor with the end of his dented pencil. "It's a blueprint of this building. If I'm looking at this right, there's another way out of here."

Gwen leans in and taps the screen. "Looks like there's something in this room that goes into the metro tunnels. A ladder?"

"That's the hope. And if this diagram is right..." Kole bends sideways to squint under the desk, and then reaches into the darkness. A moment later, a click echoes throughout the cavernous room. We all twist to face the sound. Gwen gasps. The bookshelf that houses her mother's worn paperbacks slides away from the wall to reveal a dark, empty closet. A cast iron manhole cover engraved with the letters O.K. engulfs the floor. A frosty air whistles through the cracks.

Gwen rushes over to the opening. The words that slip from her lips are almost too softly spoken to hear. "O.K. I'm okay when I'm with you."

I glance to Kole with raised eyebrows.

"It's something her dad used to say to her mom," he says quietly as he untangles himself from the chair and stands.

Gwen looks up from where she clutches the handle of the manhole cover. "Um, hello. I could use some help over here."

Kole and I help her pull the cover off the hole, metal scraping against metal. After shoving it out of the way, we stare down into a looming circle of darkness. Water trickles somewhere in the depths, and the faint rumble of a train whispers up to us. A gust of cold air swoops into the office, rustling the papers on the desk.

I nod in appreciation. "Nice one, Phantom."

"I honestly can't believe he hid this from me." Gwen shakes her head and squats beside the hole, her hair billowing around her face. "There's definitely a ladder here."

"It makes sense," Kole says. "All those times he came and went without us noticing. Plus, where does he park his car? It's not in the garage."

"He always popped in and out of his office like he'd been nowhere at all."

"But he'd have a brand new bruise on his face," Kole says.

Gwen sighs and shoves the cover back over the escape hole. "Let's stop talking about him in the past tense and get ready for tonight."

We spend the next couple of hours in preparation while the sun dips below the horizon. Snow continues to fall in a thick haze, transforming the city into a frigid wasteland. Gwen texts

Vincent from a burner phone, telling him she knows what he's done and to be ready for instructions at nine.

As soon as she hits the send button, Kole fires up the wiretap program and huddles at the desk slurping soda with headphones strapped over his ears. Gwen and I linger in the office for awhile listening in along with him, but when the silent minutes stretch into an hour, we both wander into the kitchen for some food.

She throws a frozen pizza into the oven and leans against the marble countertop. "Sorry I don't have any blood."

"It's fine. I had some earlier." I lean in and wink. "But if you're offering…"

She flushes. "Stop. I thought you said you don't drink from the neck."

"You're right. I don't." I shove away from the counter and walk over to the windows overlooking the city. From here, it looks like any other town. Quiet, calm, normal. The snow hides the blood that paints these streets.

Gwen comes up beside me. "Mind if I ask why?"

"Blood rage." I swallow. "Last time I drank from the neck, I lost control. I don't ever want to do that again."

"Are you talking about that day at the pub? When you attacked Blain Shade?"

"That was the day," I say softly. "Blain was egging me on, saying I should drink from his shifter friend. I don't know why I went along with it, but…when I tasted her blood, I snapped. I haven't had a drop from a neck since. I won't be like them, Gwen. I won't."

She touches my arm. "You aren't like them."

"Come on." I shake my head, letting out a bitter laugh. "I distinctly remember you thinking otherwise about twenty-four hours ago."

"Silas. Orpheus. Look at me."

I look down at her, and something in me tightens. She's so fucking beautiful.

She pushes up onto her toes and cups my face. "I'm sorry for what I said. I didn't mean it. You aren't like them."

"I kill people."

A conflicted expression whispers across her face. "You kill monsters."

"Doesn't that make me a monster myself?"

"I…" She shakes her head just as the timer dings for her pizza. Slowly, she backs away, before turning to grab her food out of the oven. We share a few slices on the couch, a companionable silence falling across us. Every now and then, she asks about my training, and I ask about hers. She tells me about her hopes for the city. I tell her how I wish things could be for the humans in the slums. When we're done eating, she clears her throat.

"I should go." She stands, pulling her hair back into a ponytail and exposing the delicate skin at her neck. I track her every movement. "You can stay here until it's time for you to do your part of the plan."

"I'll leave with you." I follow her into the hallway. "I want to make sure the room is ready for Vincent."

Gwen frowns. "That sounds ominous."

"Just leave this part to me."

When Vincent sees the situation in the room, he'll know we aren't joking around. Or at least that I'm not. I'll show him the sniper rifle pointed right at Four Points Pizzeria and threaten to frame him for the impending death of all the Nightshade leaders. That should be enough of a threat for him to admit the truth. He would never risk being blamed by an entire gang of angry vampires.

And if that doesn't work, I'll just threaten to shoot him in the head.

Gwen disappears into her room to change, and I wander back into the office. Kole perches at the desk with one hand on the headphones and the other on the keyboard.

"Anything yet?" I ask.

He shakes his head. "Nothing. No calls to or from anyone since Gwen texted him."

"That doesn't sound promising."

He swivels to another monitor and taps on the keyboard before a spreadsheet-type document fills the screen. "I've been taking a look at this, though. I can't get over Phantom's obsession with the Blood Market building. There are cameras everywhere, and he even has control of the refrigeration system. Why bother? Why not focus more attention on the Coils?"

"He's obsessive. You have to be in our line of work." I lean against the desk. "You don't seem to mind being regulated to desk duty."

"Trust me, I would much rather be in here than out there."

"That's definitely the smarter option. Gwen did say you're the brains."

He glances up at me. "Do me a favor though?"

"It depends on the favor."

"You've got Gwen's back, right? She can trust you?" Kole's shoulders tense. He may not be Phantom's blood, but he's certainly inherited his protective tendencies.

"Kole…if I have anyone's back, it's Gwen Kane's," I say.

He nods, his shoulders relaxing. "Yeah, I'm kind of getting that impression. Just be careful with her, okay?"

"I will," I say. "Though I'm more worried about her being careful with me. She doesn't exactly hold her punches."

Kole smiles. "That's my sister for you."

The elevator door whirs open, and Kole and I both fall silent. He pokes at the screen, and I nod along, even though I'm nodding at nothing. I clear my throat and force my eyes on the screen, not at my mate.

"What are we looking at?" Gwen asks as she joins us by the desk. I cut my eyes her way. In her tight jeans and cropped top, she looks impossibly delicious. Smooth skin, bright eyes, cheeks flushed with pink. A part of me wonders if I'm making a mistake, if I should still tell her about Nicky Tanner. I didn't kill an angel, but I still feel responsible for all of this. For her father's fate.

If tonight doesn't work, I'll tell her everything. And then I'll go back to the Saints.

"I was just showing Silas a few things, but none of it really helps." Kole clears his throat and spins in the chair. "Nothing from Vincent's phone yet."

She nods to me. "Ready to go then?"

Instead of answering, I move over to the manhole cover and help her haul it away from the underground opening. Moments later, Gwen is clamoring down the ladder with a miniature flashlight stuck between her teeth. The shadows start to swallow her whole.

"Maybe I should go first," I say.

She pauses, one hand on a rung while the other shields her eyes to glare up at me. "No way."

I sigh and wait for her to descend into the darkness before following. The metal groans when I lower myself onto the ladder. Below, Gwen's feet scrape the bottom, wherever the bottom is, and I quickly follow just in case she runs into something she can't fight alone. When I finally reach her side, Gwen sweeps her flashlight across my face. I hold up a gloved hand and blink out the stars that crowd my vision.

"Watch it," I say.

"Sorry."

"Where are we?" I glance around, but the shadows are too

thick to see more than a low curving ceiling and the vague outline of a tunnel stretching out on either side of us.

"The metro tunnels." Gwen flicks her flashlight onto the tracks below before turning the beam onto the platform. It's a thin strip of concrete, thinner than a sidewalk, and it leads in either direction from where we stand.

"Have any idea which way we should go?"

The rumble of a train shakes the ground, and a burst of cool air whips down the tunnel. A building roar echoes all around us. Gwen shouts something into the wind, but her words get snatched away before they hit my ears.

Her hand snakes out. As the ground continues to tremble, her fingers dig into my arm. Shuddering, she stares at me with wide eyes, all her earlier bravado melted away. And then it hits me. These tunnels resemble the claustrophobic streets of the slums, and the train bearing down on us only makes that sensation even worse.

Holding her against me, I press her back against the wall to shield her from the coming train. She shivers at my touch, but she doesn't resist. As the train rushes toward us, I step closer, my chest against her breasts.

With a deafening roar, the train zooms past. The air churns and pushes and throttles against us, snatching at our hair and our jackets. But in only seconds, it's over. Gwen's ragged breath is hot on my face, and her body shakes. I take a step back and drop my arm from her waist, but she snatches out a hand to stop me. With parted lips, her cheeks flood with red to erase the ghostly white.

"Orpheus." I barely hear my name over the rumble of the disappearing train.

"You're okay. I've got you."

"You always do," she whispers.

And then her lips are on mine. She winds her arms around my neck and tugs me down to her. With a groan, I push her up against the wall and spread her lips with my tongue, tasting her sweet breath. A need within me roars, a flame coaxed to life by her mouth.

Her soft hands slip up my neck and tangle in my hair. There's something so raw in the way she grips the strands in her fists. I breathe her in, driven by a need for more of this. More of *her*. Shuddering, I grip her hips and lift her from the floor, her thighs parting around my waist.

I groan as she grinds against me, my length hardening in an almost unbearable way. This is not where I had in mind when I imagined taking her for the first time, but I'm so consumed by her body flush against mine that I can only deepen the kiss. Can only dig my fingers into her hips. Can only shudder as she arches against me.

Fuck me. I want every single part of her. On my lips. On my tongue. On my cock.

I don't care where we are. I just want *Gwen*.

Suddenly, she pulls back, her face and neck so flushed, I can see the heat of them even in the darkness of this tunnel. "Wait. I don't know if we should be doing this."

"You're my mate, darling. It can't be more right than this."

"I don't want fate to decide who my mate is," she whispers.

I tense, a muscle ticking in my jaw. "I see."

Slowly, I ease her back onto the ground. Neither of us looks at each other for a good long while.

Finally, she speaks up. "You can't tell me it doesn't bother you. Some fated bond making decisions for you."

It doesn't bother me at all. Not when I can sense just how right for me she is. But she clearly doesn't feel the same, and I don't want her to see just how disappointed I am by her words.

"Look." I point to the wall just behind her head. "Phantom left a mark."

She turns and shines the flashlight on the white marking, and the beam zaps away all the tension between us. The marking matches the manhole cover's engraving, but this time, the K is criss-crossed in such a way that it looks like an arrow pointing left.

"We go that way." Gwen points down the tunnel.

We start off in silence, our boots thumping on the concrete platform. Gwen's flashlight beam bounces ahead. It highlights a rat that scurries by, a mural of intricate graffiti, and discarded shoes that reek of sweat. We don't speak. I'm not sure I can after what happened between us, and I'm not sure Gwen wants to.

The moments drag by before we reach the next ladder. The flashlight shoots a beam overhead to display another manhole cover. We both quickly scale the ladder and heave the cover aside before spilling out into a deserted side alley, the street blanketed with snow. Overhead, the night sky is hidden behind a thick layer of fog. Two abandoned warehouses squat on either side of us with their dilapidated metal sides barely clinging on like desperate silver fingers.

Gwen crunches over to a car that's parked in the alley, shielded by a black cover.

"Help me with this?" Gwen asks. The only words she's spoken since our kiss.

We each take an end and tug at the material until it falls away, revealing a junker of a car that looks like a squashed bug. Gwen frowns and glances into the driver's side window after swiping away a thin layer of condensation.

"What are you doing?" I ask her.

"Isn't it a coincidence there's a car parked in this abandoned alley? Well, there's no such thing as coincidence in my family."

She tries the door handle, and it clicks open. With a pull, the door creaks, straining against rusted hinges.

"Any keys?" I move over to the passenger side.

She rattles keys in the air along with a scrap of paper. "Phantom left this for me. It says, 'Gwen, for emergencies only'. Told you."

"Wonderful." I slide onto the faded seat. The car smells of must and stale cigarettes, but at least I won't be tempted by Gwen's coconut scent in my nose and her ass on my cock.

"Wonderful?" Gwen climbs inside and jams the keys into the ignition. "This thing is a piece of junk."

"Would you rather walk?"

"You're just happy it's not a motorcycle."

I tense. She has no idea. "You're not wrong."

She flicks her eyes at me and smiles. A real smile that sparks a light inside of me. I wish I understood what the hell is going on inside her mind, and despite every intention to keep my hands to myself, I reach over and rub my thumb across those perfect lips of hers.

She swallows, cheeks red. And then she clears her throat, turns her attention to the car, and cranks the engine. The car spurts to life and takes us Downtown, the tires churning the snow to slush.

I heave out a sigh.

Once we reach the Four Points, Gwen parks the car. We stand in the shadows of the hulking buildings and go over our plan one last time. I'll go my way, and she'll go hers. And I won't see her again until it's over.

CHAPTER 18
GWEN

The clock tower chimes out the ninth hour as I creep through the thick fog. I duck behind a green dumpster and watch my breath form ice clouds until the chimes fade. Silas must be inside the building behind the pizzeria by now. I should be there, not here on a scouting mission. My only aim is to watch and hide and wait.

Not really my strong point.

My lips throb from the ghost of Silas's lips, and I shake my head to get rid of the memory. I pushed him away, even if I regretted it the second I did. I meant what I said, though. I hate the idea of fate deciding my mate, but at the same time…he feels right. Every logical thought says otherwise. He's an assassin. Someone who hides the truth of who he is from the world. I don't even know what to call him.

And yet…

"You there?" Kole's voice blasts into my ear, and I force my thoughts away from Silas. Or Orpheus. Or whatever he is called.

It doesn't matter, really. He's the same person deep down inside.

My mate.

"Yep," I say into the phone. "I'm outside Vincent's place now."

"What do you see?" Kole's voice sounds tinny through the cheap cell. After finding a stash of my father's burner phones in the office, I took two for tonight. One for the Vincent texts and one for calling Kole. I'll toss both afterwards so that none of the Nightshade or Blackthorn vampires can trace this back to us. It's a paranoid plan, but I'd rather be paranoid than dead.

I poke my head out from behind the dumpster and squint through the fog. Vincent lives alone in a first floor apartment a few blocks south of the Four Points. It's in a stretch of two-story concrete slabs with postage stamp sized yards and stunted driveways. The lights blare through thin, gauzy curtains, and his pickup truck clogs the drive, windshields covered by a thick layer of snow. Several other cars squat behind his.

"He's home, and it looks like he's been here all day," I say.

"How can you tell?"

"Kole, have you even looked outside today?" I ask. "There's snow and fog, and approximately zero visibility."

He laughs. "I haven't left this room, and it is glorious."

"My father is going to want his office back, you know."

"I can take him."

I can't help but smile. "Good luck with that."

I edge out from behind the dumpster, glance one way down the street and then the next. No cars, no pedestrians. Just a thick white haze like cotton candy. No one wants to be out on these streets, in this weather, at this time of night. No one sane, at least. "I'm moving closer so stay quiet."

With quick steps, I cross the street and keep my head down.

My heavy boots crunch the snow, and I grit my teeth until I reach the driveway. Breath caught in my throat, I weave through the cars before ducking behind the truck to wait.

Silence whispers down the block.

I slip around the side of the truck and press my back against the building. A dog's bark erupts from nearby, as loud as a revving motorbike. I wince and wait, heart pounding. The dog barks again. This time, it sounds like it's coming from inside. I let out a long, slow breath before slinking the rest of the way to the window.

Vincent Shade sprawls across a leather couch in faded gray sweatpants and a crumpled tee as he flicks through options on his television. A shaggy dog trots over to his side and licks his hand. He gives the dog a weak smile and ruffles his fur before turning bloodshot eyes back onto the flashing screen. A few other solemn vampires stroll into the room to hand him a beer, and Blain walks over with an open pizza box. He holds up a slice, but Vincent just shakes his head.

They're treating him as if he's sick, as if he's in mourning.

Layla, I think. My stomach squeezes like a fist. No wonder Vincent has been here all day with his friends and family looking after him. His girlfriend's dead, and here we are, about to make his life a living hell. I shake my head at myself. I can't think this way. Vincent killed that angel, and he framed my father for it. Whatever he gets, he deserves. And more.

I move away from the window and retake my post behind the dumpster, wrinkling my nose. At least all those training sessions prepared me for the onslaught of rotting fish and dripping sewage water.

"I was right," I whisper into the phone. "He's definitely in there."

"Send the text," Kole says.

With a nod, I pull the other phone from my coat pocket and type the text with gloved fingers.

We know what you did. Meet us inside the building behind the Four Points Pizzeria in one hour. Top floor. Alone. If you tell anyone, we'll know.

With the other burner to my ear, I whisper to Kole. "Sent. Anything on your end?"

"Nope. He's sitting tight so far. You?"

"No, and I'm bored already."

Kole laughs. "What did you expect him to do? Run out of the house immediately?"

"Pretty much." I sigh and squat with one hand propping me up against the dumpster. The chill seeps through my gloves. "I'm going to put down the phone but keep you connected."

"Don't do anything stupid," Kole says.

"I would never do something stupid."

After carving a makeshift hole in the snow, I settle the phone onto the ground with the receiver-side facing the sky, and I turn up the volume so I can hear Kole if Vincent makes a move. Standing, I rub my hands together fast enough to start a fire and pull the hood back over my numb ears.

At least half an hour passes with me pacing from one end of the dumpster to the other. Only the occasional shadow flickers behind the curtain, and the multicolored flash of the television never stops. Vincent needs to leave soon if he's going to leave at all. Maybe I should get closer again and see if he's made a move off that couch.

Footsteps crunch down the street. My heart jolts, and I duck behind the dumpster, my knees hitting the snow. I hold my breath and listen. The crunching grows louder as slow and steady steps head right in my direction. Wet slush clings to my jeans as I shift to peer around the dumpster. But the fog blinds my view.

The crunching stops.

Silence curls toward me like a wisp of smoke.

Crunch.

The footfall sounds from the middle of the street, just on the other side of this dumpster. I don't dare make a move. I glance around the blanketed street just as a low, whistling wind swirls down the sidewalk and rustles my hood.

Crunch.

Whoever is there knows I'm here, and whoever is there knows I hear these footsteps. My lungs squeeze from the lack of oxygen, and when I drag in a gulp of air, my breath is as loud as the metro trains.

Crunch.

Do something, my mind screams. Muscles groaning, I place my palms flat on the ground and creep around the dumpster. Now I have a clear view of the street, but instead of finding the face of my stalker, all I'm met with is an empty stretch of white road with dirty footprints leading toward me.

Crunch.

My heart pounds, and sweat droplets slip down my forehead despite the freezing cold. *Hiding is what cowards do, Gwen.* Using my fists isn't in tonight's plan, but a strange lurker outside Vincent's house isn't in the plan, either. On a normal day, I'd charge out from behind this dumpster, but today isn't a normal day. Today the strange lurker could be Isolde Thorn. The vampire who killed my mother.

Crunch.

I can't take it anymore. I stand with my fists raised. Shoes crunch and clothes rustle, and a black-clad body hurtles toward me.

Quick scan of attacker: male, tall, muscled, with a black ski mask hiding his face. Just like the vampires who surrounded me and my father that night. A thought pops into my head right as his gloved fist swings at my mouth. *We're wrong.*

His fist smashes into my face, and my lip cracks. The iron tang of blood fills my mouth, and I shake my head at the piercing pain that radiates throughout my entire head. He throws another punch, but I duck down. Palms flat on the ground, I swipe out my leg, but he dodges my attack just in time.

I bounce back up and throw my left hook. He dodges the hit and shoves an elbow into my stomach. I cough and stumble back. He comes at me, but I rush out of the way. My boots skid on the slippery ground.

He moves back in and bounces on his feet. Crouching into fight-stance mode, I pull all my power to my core and whip my leg up into the air at his face. Just before my boot hits the mark, his hand snakes out to grab my ankle and knock me off balance.

My knees charge into the ground. I roll over and push up from the pavement, but my attacker grabs my neck and slams my head against the metal dumpster. Pain sparks in my head like rockets. The world spins underneath me, and my body slumps even as I scream at it to fight back. My cheek smashes against the snow, and I peer sideways at the blurry world.

I never thought I would go out like this. I never thought it would be now. My father's solemn eyes flash in my mind, and I groan. He won't be okay if I die like this. He's not even okay as it is.

Something rough scrapes against my wrists and cinches tight. A rope of some sort. A moment later, my legs get trapped together the same way, though my boots protect my skin. With waning energy, I push and pull against my binds, but they're too tight.

My attacker rolls me over, squats beside me, and frowns. "Now. What is it you think you know?"

His voice is familiar, though I can't place from where. Someone I know, someone I talk to, but my ears still ring from the hit against the dumpster, too loud for me to spark the connection.

"You're not Vincent," I finally say through a mouthful of blood.

"No, I'm not Vincent Shade. He has nothing to do with this." He pats me on the head, and I jerk away. "Stop poking around, okay?"

My voice crawls out from the deepest part of my throat. "I won't stop until Phantom is free from everything you've done to him. This is your chance to turn yourself in to the Saints before we make your life a living hell."

Whoever you are…

"A threat isn't much of a threat if you don't have anything to back it up. And from where I'm standing, all you've got is a chipped tooth."

"Why don't you go to the building behind Four Points Pizzeria and see the threat for yourself?" I lob red spit at his shoes and curl my lips into a bitter smile when it hits the mark. "Or are you too much of a coward to face Orpheus?"

My attacker stands and brushes the snow from his black pants. "The Boss wanted to take care of that problem herself."

The blood drains from my face, but I can't let him see that. "Good. You won't be smiling when he shoots her in the head."

"Empty threats again." He frowns down at me. "This is a warning, Gwen. Yes, I know who you are. This city is tough, we all know that. But if you stop causing problems, you can enjoy a normal life. Just like all the other supernaturals who stay the fuck out of our business. Stop poking around, or I'll have to kill you next time. And that is not an empty threat."

He sighs and walks away. The crunch of his boots echoes in

my ears until the sound falls to nothing. I breathe against the ground and blink the stars out of my eyes. Silas is in trouble. Whoever that was, it wasn't Vincent Shade. And he's definitely working with Isolde Thorn.

Slowly, I drag myself over to the phone. I crawl, hands still trapped behind my back, until I can press my lips to the receiver.

"Kole, are you there?" I whisper.

"Oh, thank god, Gwen." His words tumble over one another. "Are you okay?"

"I'll live." I spit out another clump of blood. "But you need to call Silas. Warn him an ambush is on the way."

"Gwen…Silas stopped answering his phone twenty minutes ago."

CHAPTER 19
SILAS

Hazy moonlight spills through the window and gleams against the sniper rifle's metallic finish. I slip my fingers into the trigger and stare down the scope at the restaurant below. Even with the thick fog obscuring the view, it's clear the restaurant is an opposite scene to last night. The shutters are closed, the lights are off, and snow weighs down the veranda's overhead checkered tapestry. It's closed tonight, and only a handful of Nightshade vampires lounge out back, drinking goblets of blood and sharing smokes. Bobby Shade is with them, but the Mad Hatter is nowhere to be seen.

Still, it might be enough to scare Vincent into submission. The loaded sniper rifle waits for action. Aiming my phone camera around the room, I snap a few photos of the scene. Once Vincent arrives, I'll add his face to the lens, and the pieces will be in place. All it will take is a single incriminating photograph delivered to Bobby Shade's doorstep, and Vincent will be doomed. Unless he agrees to tell the Saints the truth, of course.

In the distance, the clock tower chimes out the time. Ten

o'clock already. Vincent should be here by now. With a frown, I glance at my message inbox, but nothing at all from either Gwen or Kole. I check my missed calls. Again, nothing. I dial Kole's number and wait for the ringing tone, but my phone just beeps and drops the call. *No service.*

The street below is silent and still other than the occasional skulking cat, so I lean out the window to test the cell. One bar lights up in the corner of the screen, and I try Kole's number again. The line rings, and my shoulders drop with a sigh. But as the sound repeats again and again, the tension forms rock-hard knots in my neck.

Something is wrong.

Narrowing my eyes, I cross the room and press my back against the wall. I listen for any hint of company, but only silence meets my ears. The lack of sound presses in around me so tight, my bones feel on the brink of shatter.

The whisper of feet on carpet. I aim my gun at the door just as it slams open and crashes into the wall. About a dozen black-clad bodies swarm inside with guns glinting in the dull light. There are too many of them for me to fight alone. *Fuck.*

"Drop your weapon!" someone yells.

I raise my arms and drop my gun, fighting the urge to launch myself toward the sniper rifle. Not that it would do much good at such a close range, and by the time I reached it, I'd be dead.

As the bodies move closer, familiar faces I haven't seen in years stare me down. Both men and women vampires, all in black gear with the Blackthorn loyalty tattoo branded on their neck. My mother's Soldiers. Eleven of them.

That can only mean one thing. I brace myself.

My mother slinks into the room like a lion. Her bleached hair sits in soft curls atop her shoulders, but the lines of her face are slanted and sharp. Her nose slices out of her face like a knife, and her thin lips twist into a cruel smile. Long canines glint, the edges stained with fresh blood.

"Silas, my dear," she says in the icy voice I hoped to never hear again. Despite my every attempt to keep my secret identity from her all-seeing eyes, it hasn't taken long for her to find out who I become at night. I've worn my amulet during the day for most of my life, and I thought she might never know the truth about what I look like without it. But maybe she's known all this time.

"Mother," I say.

"I thought you'd be happier to see me." She waves long manicured fingers at the sniper rifle and the blood stain on the floor. "What is this mess?"

"You're the one who created the mess." The words slice through my teeth. "I'm just trying to clean it up."

"Mess?" She lets out a tinkling laugh and turns to her Soldiers for validation. They laugh along with her, though I'm not sure they understand why. "What mess?"

"Damian Kane, the man you somehow framed for murder. The impending war for the slums. And probably ten other things I don't know about."

"You know just as well as I do that I never framed Damian Kane." She smiles and slips off her red woolen coat before handing it to one of her Soldiers. Leaving only ten for me to deal with now. "Someone else may have, but I wasn't in the city. Plus, the Saints would never listen to *me*."

"Well, it was certainly someone who works for you."

"I don't control my Soldiers' every action, Silas. You know that." She sends a sharp glance to one of her female Soldiers, and the vampire tightens her grip on her raised gun. The one that points right at my face.

"I know you're behind this."

My mother shakes her head, and her curls bounce. "I'll admit, I'll reap the benefits. Which is why I've come to have a nice chat."

"Reap the benefits?" I let out a bitter laugh. "You'll never change, will you? You don't mind if the world gets caught in the filth so long as you don't get your own hands dirty."

"Get my hands dirty like you?" She slits her eyes and moves closer. "If I'm not mistaken, you were the one who killed Nicky Tanner. Not Vincent, or whoever else you're blaming. Does Gwen Kane know?"

I flinch and close my eyes. Just like always, my mother found my button less than five minutes into our confrontation. And she pushed it as soon as she could. "Of course she doesn't know. The Nicky Tanner I killed wasn't an angel. He was a vampire. And something tells me you know exactly how this weird switch-up happened."

She ignores me and turns to drag a white-gloved finger along the barrel of the rifle. "Silas, what am I going to do with you? A sniper rifle? Who were you planning to shoot?

She leans down and presses her eye against the scope. I reach out to stop her, but a Soldier edges me away with a gun stuck into my gut. Only seconds pass before my mother's lips curl into her cruel smile. "Oh, I see. What a lovely view you have here. First Nicky Tanner and now this. Are you sure you don't want to join the Blackthorns? You'd make an excellent Soldier."

"Why don't you just kill me and get it over with?" The words slip off my tongue before I can stop them. But despite the evil in that empty soul of hers, she would never kill me. Unfortunately, there are worse things than death, especially where my mother is concerned.

"It's an option I considered, but I have a better idea." She snaps her fingers, and a Soldier leaves the room. My mother smiles, and I flick my gaze to my gun on the floor. If I move fast enough, I might be able to shoot my way out of here.

The Soldier moves back into the room and heaves something inside. My throat closes up. It's a body, though the Soldier blocks who it is from sight. *Gwen*. She got Gwen. I brace myself to see Gwen's broken face, but when the Soldier drops the body to the floor, Ronan falls into view. He's breathing, but his eyes are closed, and his face is mottled with blood.

"Ronan?" My heart freezes for several beats. I throw myself forward, but a Soldier moves to block my way. "What have you done to him?"

"If you hadn't interfered, none of this would have to happen. I do hate to harm those humans in the Coils. They give us such excellent blood."

"So it was you." I take small steps closer to my gun, so small they're imperceptible to anyone else. "You threatened him."

"No, I wasn't in the city." She waves to her crew. "But yes, I've had help from my Soldiers. The most helpful of them all is busy taking care of your other friend. The pretty one."

"Gwen." I edge closer to my gun. "Vincent doesn't stand a chance against her."

"You are wrong about so many things, Silas. And you've forced my hand." She flicks her wrist at the nearest Soldier. "Do it."

The Soldier shoots Ronan. Blood arcs through the air and sprays the walls. My heart rips out of my chest, gripped by sharp stabbing fingers. Red blinding my eyes, I roar and launch toward my gun, but the nearest Soldier kicks it out of my grasp. It rockets far across the carpet, but it's too late anyway. Ronan is dead.

Dropping my head to the floor, I crawl on hands and knees to Ronan's broken body. I cradle his head in my lap, his blood seeping into my jeans. His usually kind, laughing eyes stare up at me, now blank and empty. My mother's hand lands on my shoulder, and I whirl on her with a growl.

"Get the hell away from me or I swear to god, I will rip your head off." I shake so hard, the floors beneath me rumble.

She did this. She killed the only father I've ever had.

The vampire queen glares down at me with a bitter twist to her lips, and the emptiness in her eyes shows the truth of what she is. There's nothing there. She's a blank hole of nothingness behind her mask of cruelty. Non-feeling. Non-anything. She's just a shell of a woman who takes everything that's good in the world until there is nothing left but her empire of ice. She's done it before, and she'll do it again.

"I can't let you threaten me in front of my Soldiers, Silas." Those words slither out of her mouth like a hiss, and I know what's coming next.

It won't be the first time, but it might be the last. My mother flicks her wrist, and a Soldier slowly moves closer. I cradle Ronan's head in my lap and lift my chin, refusing to cower beneath her storm.

"Do it." Her voice is ice.

The Soldier raises the weapon and shoots.

CHAPTER 20
GWEN

Cold seeps into my bones. With a grunt, I roll over onto my belly, push up to my elbows and knees, and wriggle forward with my ass in the air. Very dignified. I poke my head out from behind the dumpster and glance around the dark street. Surely in this part of town, there's a discarded razor blade hanging around somewhere just waiting for me to find it. I need to get out of these ropes.

Tires skid across the slush, and I duck back down. The car rolls to a stop at the curb, and a door flies open while the engine still chugs.

"Gwen?"

I sigh in relief. It's Kole.

"I'm over here," I say in a whisper-shout.

Kole rushes to my side and drops to the ground, his puffy jacket swishing. A frantic look crosses his face when he spots the red smeared across my lips.

"Are you okay? What's this blood?" He points to the blood on the snow. "Is that from him or from you?"

"I'm fine. Just get me untied."

"What the hell happened?" He moves behind me and tugs at the ropes. They scrape my wrists until they fall away. With a wince, I sit up and rub the tender, swollen skin. This is going to take awhile to heal.

"I got jumped." I reach down and help Kole untie the ropes around my ankles. "Whoever it was, it wasn't Vincent."

"You have no idea who it was?" Kole hops up and holds out a hand. Groaning, I pull myself up and lean against his skinny tree of a chest. My body feels as if I've been hit with a wrecking ball, and a lump the size of Mars has sprouted on my skull.

"I recognized his voice, but I can't place it." We turn toward the street and inch over to the idling car, Kole supporting me with a hand around my back. It sits there on a curb like a broken snail, green and slimy and in dire need of a wash. Dad's choice of vehicle is seriously questionable.

"What now?" he asks.

"You should go home." I steady myself against the hood of the car and wince when my brain gallops into my skull. "I'm going after Silas."

"Are you out of your mind?" He stomps over to the passenger side door and yanks it open. With a dramatic hand wave, he motions for me to get in. "I'm coming with you."

"Kole, you don't know how to fight." I cross my arms and do my best to give off my stern fighter face while ignoring the ringing in my ears." If you got hurt, I'd never forgive myself."

"Well, then make sure I don't get hurt." He moves back over to the driver's door and slides onto the torn fabric seat. With a frown, he adjusts the rearview mirror and puts the car into gear. "You coming or not?"

With a sigh, I ease myself inside. "On one condition. You wait in the car. Like a getaway driver."

Not like a getaway driver, and he knows it. If Kole stays outside, he has a better chance of staying safe, and a better chance of not getting shot. As he pulls the car away from the curb, his jaw twitches the way my dad's does when I've done something to piss him off, but I won't back down on this. I'll do anything to save Silas, if I have to. Anything but tack Kole's life in the center of a bullseye.

"Fine," he finally says with a sigh. "I'll wait in the fucking car."

Kole turns the junker toward Four Points Pizzeria. We drive past the building where Silas and Vincent were meant to meet, and I stare up at the dark third-floor windows. The heavy fog smudges the building into a blurry brown-and-red square. Getting closer is the only way to know what—and who—is waiting inside.

We park several houses down from the building, just in case someone is keeping a close watch. When Kole cuts the engine, he turns to hold my face between his palms. "Are you sure this is a good idea?"

"I have to make sure he's all right."

"You don't have to risk your life for him, Gwen."

I yank back as if I've been bitten by a poisonous spider. "I can't believe you just said that."

"He's not some helpless girl stuck in an impossible situation, Gwen. He's not another Layla Pirelli." Kole reaches for my arm as I shove open the car door. "He's dangerous. He's violent. He's Orpheus. I feel like you're forgetting all of this because of some stupid fated mate bond."

I shake my head and back out of the car. "He's more than all of that, Kole. Maybe you can't see it, but I can."

I slam the door and head down the sidewalk toward the building. As always, this block feels like a ghost town. The street lamps hold no light, and the apartment windows are lit up with nothing but moving shadows. But the lack of light doesn't mean no one's here. It never does in Towton City. I slow my steps, keep my head down, and will myself to become part of the shadows myself.

When I reach the building's front door, it's already open. The wood creaks on the hinges as it rocks back and forth in the breeze. With quiet steps, I push inside and creep up the two flights of stairs. My feet freeze on the top step. The apartment door is blasted in as if a tank has charged through. The wood is bent and scattered around the landing in thin, jagged strips. Head still ringing from the earlier fight, I edge closer to the open door and listen.

Nothing. No footsteps, no whispers, no patter of gunshots. No one is here. With a deep breath, I push into the room. A body lies crumpled on the carpet, his face and chest smeared with wet blood.

"Silas!" I rush to his side and fall to my knees. Dark blood drips from his jacket and pools on the floor next to an identical stain. His eyes are shut, and his body limp. Carefully, I lift his head and search for the wound with salty tears stinging my eyes. "Silas. Orpheus. Please be okay."

I push aside his jacket, but the shirt underneath is clean. Frowning, I lean down and press my ear to his lips. Weak breath tickles my earlobe. My throat chokes out a ragged sigh, my entire body collapsing on top of his.

He's alive. He's going to be okay.

When I push myself up, my hand snags on something attached to his neck. A black thing stuck into his skin and forming an angry red welt. I pick it off to find a long, thin needle dripping with blood. It's a dart. Someone shot him with a fucking tranquilizer dart.

And then my eyes drift to the rifle pointed out the window. I stand and look through the view. Four Points Pizzeria is painted with blood. The dead bodies of at least twenty Nightshade vampires, including Bobby Shade, are scattered across the back veranda. A lump clogs my throat. Did Silas do this? Or was it his mother?

After double-checking that Silas still breathes, I rush down the stairs to grab Kole from the car. He's not inside. Instead, he paces back and forth on the sidewalk with hands on top of his head. When he sees me running toward him, his face breaks out into a relieved smile.

"Thank god. I was about to go in there after you."

"I need your help," I say. "Silas is out cold, and I can't carry him myself."

When I take him up to the apartment, Kole barely blinks at the blood. Instead, he hauls Silas up from the floor and motions for me to get underneath one of his shoulders. Together, we carry Silas down the staircase, out the front door, and across the frosted sidewalk. Once we've laid him down in the backseat, we angle the car toward home.

LIGHT BLINDS MY CLOSED EYES. My lids flutter open to a bright morning sun pouring through the living room windows. Blinking, I push my aching body from the stiff armchair and glance over to the couch where Silas sleeps. The pillows are empty, but the vague outline of someone's body still indents the leather.

The clatter of dishes sounds from the kitchen. I pad into the room in my bare feet and a plain gray t-shirt, rubbing my swollen eyes. Silas stands at the stovetop with the kettle boiling and bacon frying in a stainless steel pan. My stomach growls.

"Hey," I say.

Silas turns, holding a spatula in one hand a goblet in the other. He's not wearing his amulet, and so he looks like Orpheus. A very tired Orpheus. Dark blue rings his eyes. His cheeks sink into the lines of his mouth, but the hint of a smile turns up his lips.

"Hey," he says. "I thought I'd make you breakfast while I drink up. Kole found some blood for me in the office. Hope you don't mind."

I ease onto the stool and prop my elbows on the kitchen island. "You seem awfully cheery for someone who got shot by a tranquilizer gun last night."

"I'm not cheery." He turns back to the stovetop and pokes at the bacon. "I just don't know how to handle what I really feel. So, I'm making you breakfast."

"You like to cook or something?"

"Or something." He flips the sizzling bacon and takes a sip of blood. "My neighbor can't really fend for herself, and if I don't cook for her every now and then, she'll just eat takeout for weeks."

Huh. Orpheus cooks for his neighbor.

I stare down at the kitchen island and narrow my focus on a little speck of white that's always been there. Some chip in the marble, some imperfection I've never fixed. Silas's life has been so different than mine. So...harsh. Last night, we meant to toss our enemies into a living hell. Instead, he got caught in the flames. Again.

"What exactly happened last night?" I ask softly. "Who shot you?"

"My mother got wind of our plan somehow, and she showed

up with an army of Soldiers." He pauses, and then grips the countertop with white-knuckled hands.

"Silas?" I hop off the stool and move to his side. "Talk to me."

His face screws up into a distorted version of itself, an abstract painting of the real thing. And then he heaves out a ragged breath. "Ronan."

"Ronan? Your friend in the slums?"

He closes his eyes. "When you upset my mother, there are consequences. She won't hurt you, not directly. She'll take something that matters. Something that's good."

Oh. My mouth drops open. The blood on his jacket, the blood that wasn't his. It must have belonged to Ronan. "I'm so sorry, Silas. I don't know what to say."

I don't even know how to wrap my head around it.

Silas turns back to the sizzling bacon and grabs the pan from the flame. Several moments pass by in silence. He moves the bacon to a plate, and then cracks some eggs into the same pan. Within moments, sizzling fills the quiet void again.

"Vincent Shade will pay for this," he finally says. "This whole thing started with him lying to the fucking Saints."

"It wasn't Vincent," I say. "It was someone else. Someone who must have had his phone."

Silas turns to me with raised eyebrows, and I fill him in on what happened during my stage of the plan. He asks about my masked attacker with the familiar voice, but there isn't much to tell him other than what little I know. Male, tall, muscular, which rules out some people, but doesn't rule out so out many more. It could be anyone.

Silas puts down the spatula, body humming with tension. "Your lip. Did he hurt you?"

I show him my chipped tooth. "He wasn't joking around."

"That fucking bastard will pay for this." Silas snags my chin with his thumb. My breath catches at the dangerous glint in his eye. "No one can hurt you and get away with it, Gwen. No one."

Warmth floods my tired bones. He sounds positively terrifying, but...it makes me feel *alive*.

He turns back to breakfast and finishes frying up the eggs. When it's ready, we sit around the kitchen island, our forks clinking against our plates. I chew on the bacon and watch Silas do the same. Every now and again, he takes a sip from his goblet, but the blood drinking doesn't unnerve me the way I thought it would.

But now that the day has dawned and Silas sits alive and well in front of me, reality sets in. We failed last night. Totally, one-hundred-percent failed. Isolde Thorn is back with a vengeance, and my father has no hope of escape. Avoiding these truths isn't going to make them any less real.

"There's something else," I say, clearing my throat. "Did you shoot all those Nightshade vampires at the restaurant?"

He stills. "What are you talking about?"

"When I found you in that room, there were about a dozen Nightshade vampires dead in the restaurant, including Bobby Shade."

Silas shakes his head and lets out a bitter laugh. "She finally did it. She took out her biggest competition. The Coils will be hers now, mark my words."

I set my fork down. "I had a feeling. What are we going to do now?"

"I don't know, Gwen." He sighs. "I really don't know."

"But we're still going to try, right? We're going to make another plan?"

Licking his lips, he glances away from me, his face wiped clean of any emotion. "I don't think so. You got hurt. It could be worse next time." He pauses. "There may be a better way to free your father from the Saints."

Eyes narrowed, I stand and move over to his side of the island. I glare at him until he turns to meet my gaze.

"I came after you last night for a reason." I take a step closer, so close our breaths mix into one invisible cloud between us. "I came after you because I don't care what you've done. I don't care how many vampires you've killed or if you're wrong or if I'm right. When I saw you lying there on that floor, hurt...it made me realize. You're my mate, and I don't want to ignore it anymore."

"Gwen." His eyes flick across my face, and he brushes a finger against my cheek. Now that he's had his blood, his eyes burn red. Full of life. Full of heat. Tension pounds between us, and everything within me begs for his touch.

Our mouths crash together. I don't know who moved first. His hands grab my thighs and pull me toward him until I'm practically on his lap. And I don't pull back, not this time. I'm not letting anything stop me from getting what I want, and what I want is Silas Thorn.

What I want is Orpheus.

His lips taste like iron. I moan, wrapping my arms around his neck, hiking my leg around his stool, and slipping my tongue into his mouth. His length goes hard against me, and I can't think straight anymore.

Our lips move in sync, tasting, nibbling, exploring. This isn't a soft kiss. It's hard and fast and full of need. It's the kind of kiss that screams of pent-up desire. Orpheus slides his hand around my back and feels the curves of my ass. After a moment, he shudders and pulls back.

His red-tinged eyes sweep across my face. "We should do this somewhere else. Kole could walk in at any moment."

Breath catching, I nod.

Orpheus lifts me from the floor and carries me into the bedroom. He kicks the door shut behind us. More gently than I expect, he carefully lowers me onto the bed and drops a kiss onto my lips. Soft, tender, sweet. It's the total opposite of the kiss in the tunnel, where we practically dry-humped while a train barrelled past.

So, I'm not quite sure how to take this different side of him.

There are a lot of words I can use to describe Orpheus. Some of my favorites in the past have been dangerous, violent, brutal. He takes down his enemies without a shred of guilt. I'm beginning to think some of that has been for show. A way to protect himself from the world. From me.

"I want to see your body." He eases on top of me, holding himself up with fisted hands on either side of my head. "I want to taste every inch of you. And I want to make you come so many times that you'll be satisfied for days."

His words thrill me. I've never had anyone talk to me like this. Hell, I've never even had a man make me come. My hands have done all the work in the past, and my entire body hums with the anticipation of feeling someone else between my thighs. And not just anyone. *Him*. The one I've dreamed about, I'm no longer ashamed to admit.

During my quietest of moments of the past few days, I've laid on this very bed fantasizing about him, about his touch, about his tongue, about his canines against my neck. I pressed my fingers between my thighs and sighed, letting my imagination get the better of me. And I told myself that it didn't mean anything.

But I was wrong.

I fantasized about my mate because I want him.

Ache for him.

I look up at him. His dark hair curls wildly across his forehead after a night spent on my couch. And in the darkness of my bedroom, I suddenly feel exposed to him, like he can see through all my defenses and into my heart. Like he can hear the way it batters against my ribcage, betraying every emotion churning inside me, showing him that I can barely stand to look at him without falling apart.

"Orpheus," I whisper.

"I know." He drops his forehead to mine. "I've got you. We can stop right now, if that's what you want."

"What I want is you." I spread my legs and wrap one thigh around his waist.

He leans into me and steals hot kisses across my chest, his deft hands lifting my t-shirt over my head. My skin is abuzz, my body humming. My senses feel ten times more heightened than they usually do. He unclasps my bra, and then his mouth is on my breasts, and oh my god, I could scream out in ecstasy just from this.

His tongue teases my nipple, sliding against its hard, erect mound. How can this alone feel so impossibly good?

With a frenzy I didn't know I had, I reach down to his jeans and fumble with his belt. I need it off. I need his cock. I want him inside me *now*.

"Is someone in a hurry?" He pauses, his lips seductively close to my nipples. He gazes up at me from between my breasts, and it's the sexiest thing I've ever seen in my life.

"Little bit," I say in a whisper. "The ache is so bad I think I might explode."

"Oh, you're going to explode all right." He moves his hand to his belt and helps me unbuckle it before standing and sliding off his jeans.

I gasp. I didn't think he could be quite this…big.

"Your turn." He removes my panties and tosses them onto the floor.

I'm naked. One-hundred percent naked. Before now, the only person to see me naked was...well, me. And now I'm spread open in front of Orpheus. It makes me burn with desire, especially when I see the appreciative look in his eyes.

"You're so fucking sexy." He climbs back on top of me. "I could spend hours ravishing your body."

His words send tingles along my skin.

"You're the sexy one." I drag my fingers along the ridges of his stomach, relishing in each dip around his abs, letting my hand linger on the carved V leading down to his cock. It's so hard it's bulging, clearly eager to be inside me.

It makes me feel alive, confident, powerful.

In fact...

With a smile, I flip him over. He's heavy and huge, but he's not putting up a fight, so it makes it easy for me to pin him on the bed. His eyes widen, and a delicious smile spreads across his lips. I can see that I've surprised him, but in the best possible way.

"Well, well, well," he murmurs. "Do what you want with me, Gwen Kane. *Anything* you want."

Even though I've never done this before, I'm not a prude, and I know how this works. I lift my hips and drag my hand up the length of his cock, from the base all the way to the swollen tip.

"You're driving me crazy," he groans and shifts his cock even closer. "I've wanted you for so fucking long."

I lick my lips and straddle him, guiding his head closer to the apex of my thighs. "Does that mean I shouldn't stop here?"

"Fuck no." He lifts his hips, and the tip of him brushes against my wetness, making me shudder. "Never stop."

And then he enters me, my walls expanding to take him in. A

million sensations pass through me at once. The way I slide against him. The way our hips join as one. The way his eyes burn through me. I grind against him, and he hits the very back of me, causing me to drop back my head and moan so loud, my voice echoes through the apartment.

"You feel so fucking good." He meets my hips with his own, hands locked tight around my waist. With a moan, I palm his chest so I can take him deeper.

Delicious pleasure shudders through me.

I rock against him. My fingernails drag down his skin, leaving marks behind. It's evidence of my need for him and the overwhelming pleasure that builds so fast—too fast—for me to handle.

Before I can slow down, I'm screaming out his name. An explosion rocks through me, leaving me breathless, panting, and dripping with sweat. And at the sound of my pleasure, Orpheus isn't far behind. He roars as I shake around him, coming inside of me with one final thrust.

It's pure, exquisite bliss.

And I never want it to end.

CHAPTER 21
SILAS

While Gwen showers, I pace in the living room. I can't keep this up. I should have told Gwen about Nicky Tanner's death first thing this morning, but when she called me her fucking mate…

Everything is different now. She looks at me, and there's a light shining in her eyes. I've tasted her skin. I've buried myself inside of her. And when she knows what I've done, that light will twist into darkness.

Gwen, I think, *I killed someone named Nicky Tanner. I'm going to turn myself in.*

My tongue is as rough as sandpaper. Gwen returns to the living room in an oversized t-shirt, drying her hair with a towel. God, she's fucking gorgeous. Her cheeks are still flushed from sex. If only all of this could go away. If only I could spend hours pleasuring her on her bed.

We could build a life together. For the first time in my life, I can see a future that isn't marred by darkness and death.

But it's time. I can't keep this from her any longer.

"Gwen," I say.

A ding-dong reverberates throughout the apartment. Gwen turns toward the sound. "Bit early for visitors."

Ding-dong.

Gwen pads out of the room to check the door. When she's gone, I suck in a deep breath and exhale it just as slowly. Maybe there's a chance she won't hate me. She said she doesn't care how many vampires I've killed. The supernatural I killed *was* a vampire. Maybe she'll understand that all I did was pull the trigger one night, just like always. I never knew it would lead to this.

A few moments later, Gwen returns with a brown envelope in her hands. The sharp, slanted handwriting on the label leaps up like a coiled snake. I shove away from the island, grab the package from Gwen's hands, and toss it into the trash can before she can blink.

"What the hell, Silas?" She frowns and lifts the package back out of the trash.

"You don't want to open that."

"I think I'll decide what I do or do not want to open for myself, thanks."

"That's my mother's handwriting."

"Oh, I see." She frowns and pokes the package with her pinky. "It's not big enough to be a bomb."

"My mother would never send a bomb." I reach out a hand, and this time, she lets me drop the package into the trash where it joins the cracked egg shells from breakfast. It can rot there. "Whatever this is, it's worse."

Gwen paces back and forth in front of the trash can, her bare feet squeaking on the tiled floor. "This is stupid. I'm not going to be afraid of a package."

Before I can stop her, she snatches up the package and rips it open. She stuffs her hand inside, and I grit my teeth. It's going to be someone else's skin. Or worse. With furrowed eyebrows, Gwen slides a CD out of the envelope's depths with a yellow Post-It note stuck to the front that reads, *Play me.*

I should be relieved, but I'm not. This seems much more ominous than skin.

"I don't like this," I say as I follow Gwen down the hallway toward her bedroom. "She's playing a game. One she won't win if you snap that CD in half and throw it away."

"I have to know what this is," she says, but her voice shakes.

She strides into her bedroom and puts the CD into her laptop. The file automatically opens, and my mother's voice slithers out of the speakers.

"If I'm not mistaken, you were the one who killed Nicky Tanner. Not Vincent, or whoever else you're blaming. Does Gwen Kane know?"

"Of course she doesn't know."

All the blood drains from my face as I fix my gaze on Gwen's stiff back. Heart slamming against my ribcage, a tinny ringing fills my ears. Every inch of my monstrous self wants to take back every moment of the past few days just to stop it all from leading to this one single moment when my mother rips the world out from under my feet.

Gwen never should have heard it this way. But she does, and she turns, and her eyes are as hard as this building's steel case exterior.

"You." Her shoulders shake. A tear slips down her cheek. "You did this."

"Gwen." I hold up my hands. "This isn't as bad as it sounds."

"You killed Nicky Tanner!" Her scream bounces off the walls and slams against my eardrums. She grabs a book from her desk and hurls it across the room where it hits the wall by my face with a loud smack.

I close my eyes. I can't look at her, not anymore. "You're right. I did."

She roars and another smack sounds by my ear. When I open my eyes, she paces vicious circles in the far corner of the room, her fists clenched tight at her sides and her face as red as blood. My heart rips in half. I've broken her. I've turned her into me.

"The Nicky Tanner I killed was a vampire, not an angel. And I may have pulled the trigger, but I didn't frame your father, Gwen. With everything that's happened, you have to realize that."

She stops pacing and hisses at me through clenched teeth. "The only thing I realize is that you're a fucking liar."

"I was going to tell you." I step inside the room and brace my body for her attack. But I have to make her understand. "When you ran into me at the cathedral yesterday, I was there to turn myself in."

She laughs. A high-pitched sound devoid of any real humor. "I can't believe anything you say. Not anymore."

"I'll prove it to you," I say. "I'll go to the angels now, and it'll all be over."

"Yeah?" She wipes the tears off her face with shaking fingers. "Well, then go do it."

I hesitate. I don't want to leave everything broken this way. If I do this, I'll never see her again. "Gwen, is there any way—"

"Do it!"

Gwen glares at me in a way she never has before. Not even when she thought I was a murderer with no soul. There is nothing but pure hatred etched into the deep lines of her crumpled face. I slowly back toward the bedroom door and give her one last glance before I go. She does not say another word. Neither do I.

❧ ❧ ❧

WHEN I REACH THE STREET, I shove through a cluster of reporters loitering outside Gwen's home. They must have found out Damian Kane is Phantom, and his execution is in two weeks. They'll harass Gwen until it's over.

Someone sticks a microphone into my face, and I fight the urge to bite off the black styrofoam and spit it on the ground.

"Silas Thorn." The reporter's high-pitched voice grates against my eardrum. "Are you involved with Damian Kane's daughter?"

Another reporter jogs beside me. "Did he really murder an angel? Was she involved?"

"Excuse me." I stop short and turn my eyes toward the camera before clearing my throat. A microphone pops into my face with the label, *The 24/7 News*. That will do just fine. "I'm on my way to the Saints to turn myself in and prove Damian Kane is innocent."

Several lightbulbs flash, and the reporters shout questions over themselves, jostling elbows and shoulders to get closer. But I've said everything I need. The news will spread fast, and Gwen will see I meant every word I said, not that it will make any difference now.

The reporters trail after me as I hike the few blocks from Gwen's apartment to the cathedral, my boots sloshing in the slush. Several of the more intrepid ones shout questions at my back as they lug their cameramen behind them, but most fall silent or whisper amongst themselves. Just as I hit the corner, a black sedan with dark-tinted windows rolls up beside me.

I keep walking with my head down and hands tucked in my pockets. The car sloshes at my side and curves down the road on pace with every step I take. Narrowing my eyes, I feel for my gun. It isn't here. Mother must have taken it when she knocked me out last night.

The engine roars. Tires squeal on the pavement as the car hurtles onto the sidewalk, slicing sideways in the slush to block my way. I stiffen and brace myself to run when the passenger-side door swings open. A black-clad Blackthorn vampire named Craig Martinez chews a wad of gum and spits it at the ground. And he holds a military-grade machine gun, aimed straight at me.

A reporter screams, and the shutter click of cameras fills the air.

"Get into the car, Silas." He gives an almost imperceptible nod to the backseat. I take a slow step back, and he clicks his teeth with a slight head shake. If I get inside that car, I'll never make it to the Saints. But even if I try to run, I won't get far. Craig Martinez isn't known for losing what he's ordered to find.

After sliding across the leather seat, I slam the door behind me. The locks tumble only seconds later. The car revs and pulls off the sidewalk, reporters chasing after us until they fade into tiny specks in the rearview mirror. Between me and the front seat, a clear bulletproof sheet of glass shields Craig and the driver from anything I could throw at them.

Even though I recognize Craig, I don't recognize the driver. Many members of Blackthorn disappeared in the years following my mother's banishment. Several stuck around long enough to keep the business going, but Damian Kane didn't make it easy for them. Mother will have some new crew members now.

The car slides through Uptown, past the elegant post-war townhouses of Royal Hill and Diamond Bay until we reach a scattering of newer warehouses with an uninhibited view of the river. The tires crunch on gravel as we pull to a stop outside an unmarked white-paneled building. No doubt this is unlisted and off-the-books, and there's no telling what it's for. Probably blood or drugs.

Craig climbs out of the car, opens my door, and pokes my knee with the machine gun. With a sigh, I step outside just as my mother exits the open warehouse door. A tailored white suit hugs her frame, and pearl earrings dangle from her ears. Craig pokes me in the back without a word, and I make the short trek to where she stands waiting.

"Hello, Silas," she says, not even bothering with a cruel smile. There's no pretense of friendliness today. "You're wearing that Orpheus mask again."

I left my amulet back at Gwen's.

"This is the real me, I'm afraid."

She tsks. "What the hell did you think you were up to this morning? You spoke to a *reporter* about turning yourself in?"

"It's time I take responsibility for my actions."

"Not at my expense. Turning yourself in means clearing Damian Kane's name, which means scrutiny will be back on me. Or worse." She snaps her fingers, and Craig sticks the barrel of the gun in my back. "Will you go willingly?"

"Go willingly where?"

"You want to be locked up? Fine, I can give you a version of that. Take him inside, boys. Cage number three."

CHAPTER 22
GWEN

I narrow my eyes and aim my fists at the punching bag. Only one face imprints itself on my mind this morning. One with a broad jaw, and sharp cheekbones, and a twisted smile to match. Silas Thorn.

Punch.

Orpheus.

Punch.

My mate.

Punch. Punch. Punch.

Gritting my teeth, I slam my fist into the bag again and again until my knuckles throb. After a quick splash of water on my sweat-drenched face, I throw myself at the bag again, but it doesn't take long for Silas's face to fade and the punches to hurt no one but myself. With a sob, my arms drop to my sides and I slide to the mat with my hands in my hair.

How could he do this to me? I trusted him.

Kole finds me an hour later with my chin on my knees and my arms wrapped tight around my legs. Tears prick the corners of my eyes but I blink them away. There's no reason to cry anymore. Silas agreed to turn himself in. Soon, my father will be free to come back home. What's wrong with me?

"Are you okay?" Kole hovers on the edge of the mat, showered, and dressed for the day, which probably means it's well past noon. I've missed work. Again.

"No, not really." I stand from the mat and take a weak swing at the punching bag, but it only sways an inch. My tears have doused the raging fire, and there's no fight left in my bones.

"I just turned on the TV to watch the news about some slum protests, but there's another story blowing up right now." He holds open the door. "You're going to want to see this."

"Does it have to do with Silas Thorn?" I stride across the mat and follow him down the hallway.

"Actually, yeah, it does."

I stop. "Then I don't want to see it."

"Trust me, Gwen. You do." He grabs my hand and drags me into the living room.

The 24/7 News scrolls across the screen, flashing a photograph of Orpheus. Not Silas. He must have done it after all. He actually went to the Saints. With my eyes glued to the screen, I perch on the edge of the couch and ball my hands in my lap.

"This is a sign that Towton City needs a stern hand to guide it. Someone willing to stand up to the organized vampire gangs rather than bend to their will. When someone can be abducted in broad daylight in front of a group of witnesses, we just can't continue to ignore what our city has become." The news reporter shuffles her papers and frowns into the camera. "Even out here in No Man's Land, we deserve better than this."

"What?" I turn to Kole with a gasp.

"It's all over the news." Kole punches the remote control to turn up the volume. "A car rolled up by Silas about two blocks away from here. They had guns. There's a video and everything. Look, they're about to play it again."

My hands grip each other when the video plays. Silas looks into the camera, and when he speaks, it's as if he's speaking to me.

"I'm on my way to the Saints to turn myself in and prove Damian Kane is innocent."

Then, he turns and walks away. The video feed follows along and moments later, a car shrieks to a halt on the sidewalk. A vampire holding a massive gun says something to Silas, but a piercing scream drowns it out.

"What happened?" I ask Kole, my eyes still frozen on the screen in case there's more to the video. "Who was that?"

"Craig Martinez. Rumored to be a Blackthorn Soldier, but no one's seen him for awhile."

"So, the Blackthorns took him." I push up from the couch and pace back and forth in front of the TV. The station starts to play the video again, but I've seen enough. Isolde Thorn won't stop until she's broken everyone, even her only real family.

"Looks that way." Kole props his legs on the coffee table and leans back in the armchair, as if today is just another day, as if we're casually chatting about the weather instead of Silas getting abducted by his own mother. "Good riddance. Let her deal with him instead of us."

I whirl on Kole with narrowed eyes. "He was on his way to clear my dad's name. If he's being held at gunpoint, he can't exactly do that now."

"He only said that to get away from you." He punches the mute button. "I still can't believe you let him go."

"Did you not see the video just now? He was really going to do it."

Kole shakes his head and frowns. "I can't believe it. You're actually worried about this guy."

"You know what?" I cross my arms. "I *am* worried about Silas. He just got abducted by a monster, probably because she found out he wanted to turn himself in. Now, she'll never let him clear my dad's name. She might even kill him."

Kole launches off the chair and strides toward me. He's never looked at me like this before, with downturned lips and narrowed eyes. He jabs a finger at the TV and it rattles on its stand. "Just because he said he was turning himself in doesn't mean he was going to. I can't believe after everything he's done, you still trust him."

I take a step back. "I don't still trust him."

"Yes, you do." Kole points at the screen. The video plays the moment Silas walks out the front door, head down, and eyes zeroed in on his feet. "If you didn't, you never would have let him walk out of here. You would have taken him to the Saints yourself."

Kole and I never argue, but this feels horribly like an argument to me. I spin away from him and sink into the couch to watch another replay of the Silas video. There's some truth in what Kole says, but every time the Blackthorn vampire points the machine gun at Silas's heart, my own freezes mid-beat.

"Why are you giving me such a hard time about this?" I ask.

"Because ever since you two teamed up, your choices have been seriously questionable."

On the video feed, the gun points at Silas, and he climbs into the car. The door slams, and they disappear down the street, the tires rolling tracks into the melting snow. He made a choice to go with those vampires, but that was the only choice he had.

"It's not a choice when there's no other option." I close my eyes. "He's my mate, Kole."

"There's always another option."

KOLE and I spend the rest of the day on non-speaking terms, especially after I try calling Alaric and can't get an answer. I don't leave the apartment, but he doesn't either. Instead, we both sprawl out in the living room with our eyes attached to the news. Several times I open my mouth to speak, but then I can't find the words. I'm not sorry, and I don't regret anything I've done.

Elliott and Eric show up around four after a day spent canvassing the city again. I buzz them in, and we gather in the living room to continue staring at the screen. Eric and Kole share the couch, while Elliott and I take an armchair each.

Elliott frowns at the TV when they replay the Silas video. "Everyone in the city is talking about this. They think it's connected to Isolde Thorn being back."

"Well, they're not wrong," Kole says.

With a sigh, I turn off the news. I've had enough for the day. Nothing else has happened in hours, and my eyes might bleed if I watch the reporters go over the same thing twenty more times. "We need to do something."

Elliott's fingers find her pearls. They slip back and forth while she gives her brother a look. *Whoosh, whoosh, whoosh.*

I narrow her eyes at her. "What's going on?"

"Elliott is still getting those calls," Eric says with a frown. "She got five more today when we were out canvassing."

"It was a woman's voice this time," Elliott says softly. "Sounded familiar. When I let Eric listen in, he recognized it from the news. Isolde Thorn."

"Fucking hell," I say. "Isolde Thorn is quickly becoming the bane of my existence."

It was like this once before. Every bad thing that happened in Towton City could be traced back to her, but only in whispers and vague connections and a leftover whiff of sweet perfume. Never in a way that proved anything.

I push up from the armchair with a groan. All the bruises from last night have hardened into painful balls, and my hands ache from my earlier punching bag incident. Last night, I stayed awake watching Silas's shallow breaths, just in case the tranquilizers did more than knock him out. I got maybe two hours, tops, before the rising sun interrupted my dreamless sleep.

But there's no rest for the wicked, I suppose. Because the other wicked ones refuse to rest.

"Right." I say. "Let's head to the office and see what we can do. Kole, I could use your help…"

My heart feels wrong with this wall up between us. Kole and I need to put aside whatever fight we're having. We've always been in sync, and I don't feel like myself without him.

There's a pause before he answers, but then his voice slides out sure and strong. "I'm on it."

We set up shop in the office, and Kole fires up the workstation. After several moments of clicking around, he turns to me. "So, what are we looking for?"

I tap a pencil against the monitor. "Can we search for anyone who has the last name Thorn?"

Kole types in the search request, and the program pops out only one other name: Silas.

"Should I…?" Kole clears his throat.

"Yeah, go on."

Kole clicks on his name, and the information fills the screen. Just like his mother's entry, the program only shows patchwork details. The address and phone number sections are blank.

There's one photo of him taken four years ago, and he's wearing that amulet of his. It's not his real face.

Still, my heart lets out a painful beat.

"Wait a minute." Eric leans over Kole's shoulder to point at the monitor. "Is this what I think it is?"

"If you think it's a highly-detailed report on everyone in this city, then yeah, it's what you think it is."

"Are we all in here?" Elliott asks.

"I'd be surprised if you weren't," I say.

Kole closes out the program and turns to me. "Unfortunately, this is useless. There's nothing in here."

I frown. "There has to be something. My father left us that code for a reason. And it's not just so we could use the hidden exit. He must have something on this computer that can help."

"Oh." Kole's eyes widen. "*Oh.*"

Eric grins. "He's got that look on his face."

"Out with it, Kole," I say, but my heart is in my throat. Kole has found something, something that may help us stop Isolde Thorn once and for all. I can tell by the sharp glint in his eye.

Kole leans back in the swivel chair and laces his hands behind his head. "Your father hacked into the Blood Market building. I kept looking at it, wondering why he would do that, but now it makes sense. We have cameras to monitor it, but it goes a lot deeper than that. From here, we can lock all the doors, turn off all the lights, and shut down the refrigeration system that keeps the blood cold. That's why he gave us that code. He wants us to shut her down."

"Wait a minute. Are you saying we can shut down the Blood Market?" Eric asks with a gasp.

"Do it." I stab my finger at the screen. "Do it right now. If she doesn't have access to the Blood Market, she's fucked."

"The vampires will riot against her if they can't get to their blood." Eric grins. "She'll have to give in to whatever we demand."

"I don't like this guys..." Elliott whooshes her pearls back and forth, glancing from me to Kole to Eric and then back to me again. "You're just going to make her mad."

"Gwen," Kole says with a smile. "You make the call."

"Do it," I say with fisted hands. "Let's hit her where it hurts."

CHAPTER 23
SILAS

Three cages the size of prison cells litter one corner of the empty warehouse. Craig pokes me in the back with his gun until I stand before the largest of the metallic collection. Inside, a pristine twin mattress sits amongst a perfectly-aligned stack of my childhood toys. One of these is the unopened Lego set my mother gifted me on my ninth birthday when she lifted me out of the slums. As her *apology*.

I don't know what game she's playing.

A vampire with a face like a squashed rat slides open the rattling cage door. He nods at Craig, tosses him the keys, and shuffles toward the warehouse exit. The soles of his shoes scrape against the floor and echo off the steel walls until he disappears into the sunlight.

"Go on in, Silas," Craig says. "Stop stalling."

"Are you really going to do this?" I arch my brows. "Put me in a cage?"

He shrugs and twitches the barrel of the gun toward my face. "Orders. I do what I'm told."

I step inside the cage and face him. "I remember a time when you wouldn't have followed these orders."

"And I remember a time when you would have gone in without arguing." He slides the rolling cage door shut and twists the key in the deadbolt. "Just do what she says. I don't know how much patience she has with you anymore. She might stop holding back."

A hard laugh bubbles up in my throat. "You don't actually think she holds back, do you?"

"I know she holds back." He attaches a strap to his gun, and the weapon slips to his side like a sling. "If she didn't hold back, you'd be dead."

With a sigh, I sit on the mattress and drop my elbows to my knees. Craig turns to face the warehouse doors with arms crossed over his chest. He's actually going to stand guard, though against who or what it's hard to say. No one will be coming after me.

He didn't start out this way. Not long after I turned twelve, Craig Martinez stood up for the owner of a laundromat near the Four Points who felt threatened by the Nightshade vampires. The shifter just wanted to live his life, but his business sat squarely inside their territory, and they wanted to make it theirs. Craig watched and waited, skulking in the shadows and biding his time. And the next time a Nightshade dropped in on the laundromat, he made sure to break enough bones to prove a point.

He clearly wouldn't do that now. My mother got her claws into his soul. When you're surrounded by monsters, there's nothing to stop you from becoming one yourself.

●●●

I DON'T KNOW how much time passes before Craig finally leaves the warehouse. As soon as his shadow disappears outside, I turn to the toys on the ground. He'll be back, and he'll be back soon, but there must be something here to help me escape.

My mother has left an odd assortment of toys. In addition to the Lego set, the cage contains a box of green army soldiers, a race car collection, and a board game called Mouse Trap. Cars, soldiers with guns, and a cage.

"Always trying to be clever," I mumble under my breath.

I take a few of the army soldiers with the sharpest edges and slide them into my pockets. It isn't much, but I might be able to shove them down someone's throat. Or better, stab the sharpest edges into their windpipe. Just as I'm reattaching the lid to the box, Craig enters the warehouse with a bag of blood, the key ring on his belt jingling with each step.

"If you're trying to look for a weapon, I wouldn't bother."

"Just feeling sentimental."

Craig snorts and holds the bag through the bars. "Here, got you some lunch."

Edging over to the bars, I eye the key ring on his belt. It would be easy to snatch it if I caught him off guard, but I can't make a move now unless I want it to be my last. He knows exactly what I'm thinking, and the stone in his eyes almost dares me to follow through.

With a twisted smile, I take the blood. "Thanks, Craig."

"Smart choice."

I drop the blood on the floor, leaving it to rot. I move to the bed and stare at the blank walls. I pace circles around my cage. Minutes stretch into hours and hours blur into a meaningless jumble of time.

I must have fallen asleep when the click of my mother's heels stabs my eardrums. I stay frozen on my bed and refuse to crack open my eyes. If she thinks I'm asleep, then maybe she'll go away.

"He's been fine, Boss." Craig's voice rumbles across the empty warehouse. "No need to check on him yourself."

"Oh, him." Her voice has an edge to it. "Is he awake?"

"He's been asleep for about an hour."

"Good." She lowers her voice into a harsh whisper. "Someone has stolen my Blood Market."

A shuffle, a throat clear. "What do you mean?"

"They've locked me out. The refrigerator system is off. All that blood is gone."

"Who the fuck did that?"

"Gwenyth Kane."

My body tenses, and a slow smile spreads across my face. Gwen stole my mother's Blood Market? If she shut down the systems and locked the door…

Well fucking done, Gwen Kane.

"Question him and make him tell you everything. I only just got my market back from those idiot Nightshade vampires. I won't let her take it from me."

"No problem, Boss."

"And Craig, use whatever means you deem necessary. I sent you a text with some helpful information."

"Of course."

After my mother's heel click fades, Craig rolls open the cage door and steps inside. I'm on my feet in seconds, ready for him. Craig throws back his shoulders, pushes up his sleeves, and cracks his knuckles. "You hear all that, Silas?"

"Every glorious word. And unfortunately for you, I have no idea how she did it."

"Sure you don't." He folds his arms over his chest. "Protecting her won't do either of you any good. If you don't tell me, someone else will, and I don't think you want the Boss to go after one of Gwen's other friends."

"She wouldn't." But that's a lie. That fits my mother's style to a T.

"Let's see." Craig sticks a tongue out between his teeth as he pokes at his cell phone. "Elliott Edwards. She was seen going into Gwen's house this morning right around the time Gwen shut down the Blood Market. If you don't talk, the Boss will bring this girl in. And she will be questioned sharply."

"Elliott Edwards is a pacifist who wouldn't hurt a slums rat. How can you be okay with torturing someone like that?"

"If you talk, I won't have to."

"I don't know anything, Craig."

"I find that hard to believe. You two have been up each other's asses for days."

I narrow my eyes. "The last time I saw Gwen Kane, she threw books at my face. Any plans to steal the Blood Market, she didn't confide in me."

"All right." He motions for me to move closer. "I don't want to do this, Silas, but you're giving me no other option."

"There's always another option."

He hurls his fist at my face.

CHAPTER 24
GWEN

The victory doesn't feel quite as sweet as I thought it would. Elliott was right. Taking a shot at Isolde Thorn doesn't actually solve much. Sure, now she's shit out of luck without her Blood Market, but she still has all the humans in the Coils. And my father is still stuck in the cathedral dungeons. Locking up the market was revenge, plain and simple. It wasn't justice.

After we stole the market, Elliott and Eric headed back to their shared apartment. Eric's convinced the whole thing is over. Elliott…well, Elliott was still pushing her pearls around her necklace when they descended to the streets below.

"Gwen, have you seen this stuff about the protest?" Kole stretches out on the couch under a thick comforter, back on speaking terms with me. Outside, the moon curves like a fingernail in the cloudless sky, and the windows fog against the stinging chill.

I peer over my dog-eared paperback at the news. "Is that still going on?"

"It's doing better than that. It's growing."

He's right. This morning, ten slum residents stomped around outside the slums, protesting against the vampires. Now, at least fifty wave hand-painted signs at the news cameras while chanting cheers about their cozy little slice of the city. They want the vampires to leave them alone, but they don't want to find another home.

"Good for them," I say. "Though calling the slums cozy might be a bit of an overstatement."

Kole chuckles and lobs a newspaper ball at the trash can in the corner. It nicks the little spot it always does and drops into the basket with a *plunk*. "Two points."

"And the crowd goes wild." I pump my fists in the air.

Kole's smile falls away as he meets my eyes across the room. "Gwen, I'm sorry about earlier."

"You know what? I am, too."

"Let's never fight again."

"Deal."

Kole cracks a smile, and I shoot one back, though it strains me to do so. My mind stutters over everything still wrong, and smiling feels like a betrayal to my father, to Elliott, and even to Silas.

"We interrupt our slums protest coverage for breaking news. Andrea, to you."

I sit up straighter in the armchair and drop my book to my lap.

"Thanks, Mark. Towton City, I'm coming to you live from the home of Elliott Edwards, famous for encouraging the humans of the slums to protest against the vampires. As you can see behind me, a vicious fire has spread quickly. Many residents call this building home. So far, we don't know how many have made it out alive."

My knees dig into the hardwood floor in front of the TV, but I didn't know I moved.

"Kole?" My voice cracks.

"I'm calling them now, Gwen." He shoves his phone to his ear and paces circles around the coffee table.

Ding-dong. That sound sends a bucket of ice down my spine. My head pivots on my neck, inch by horrifying inch, until I am gazing at the living room's doorway, and just beyond it, the elevator.

"No." I stare at the metallic doors and will the sound to disappear. "This isn't happening."

Ding-dong. A hollow ringing fills my ears. Standing, I move over to the doorway with my eyes glued to the elevator. If I never answer the door, I won't have to know what's down there waiting for me. I won't have to know if it's something else from Isolde Thorn.

"Gwen, they're not answering." Kole stabs his phone and redials immediately.

"I'll be right back..."

A numbness consumes me. My feet move forward. I ride the elevator downstairs, open the front door, and look down. A small brown package wrapped in a neat red bow sits on the steps. The label says my name and nothing else, and the handwriting is an exact match to the package sent this morning.

When I return to the living room, I hold the package with the very tips of my fingers as if it's a ticking bomb about to obliterate us at any moment.

"What is that?" Kole asks with the phone still clutched to his ear.

"I don't know." I place it on the coffee table and back away.

"Is it from..."

"Yes."

"Are you going to open it?"

"I don't know."

Kole frowns and pulls the phone away from his ear. "Do you think it has something to do with Silas?"

"No." I suck in a deep breath to brace myself for the words I'm about to say. "I think it has something to do with the fire."

"The fire?" Kole drops to his knees and places trembling fingers on the top of the package. "I'll open it."

"Kole, are you sure you—"

He cuts me off with a glare. "If it's about Eric and Elliott, I'm opening it."

He rips open the package. Inside sits a matchstick. Deep black curls up the thin wooden stick, and when he lifts it from the box, the tip shatters into ash. A piece of paper sits beneath it.

Kole holds up the paper, and the charred specks rain down on the table. "Give me back my market."

The ringing in my ears grows louder until all I can hear is a high-pitched scream. The world tilts, and I sit hard on the floor. Kole slams his phone to his ear, and a moment later, my head clears enough for me to make out the words his mouth creates.

"Thank god, Ells. Are you okay?" He jams his free hand into his hair.

My shoulders release the tension. Elliott's okay. But as he nods along to whatever Elliott says, his face transforms. Silent tears race down his face, and when he opens his mouth to speak, no sound escapes from his curled lips.

"Kole?" I slide across the floor to his side. "Kole, what's wrong?"

He drops the phone to the floor where it explodes into a dozen pieces.

"You're scaring me," I say in a whisper.

I jump when my own phone rings. Without even looking at the display, I answer. "Ells?"

Soft sobs filter through the cell. "She killed him, Gwen. My brother is dead."

THE WORLD no longer feels real. Kole refuses to speak. He sits minute after minute and hour after hour on the floor. His back presses against the window's cold glass as he stares a hole into the spot where his newspaper balls hit the wall. I drape a blanket across his legs and move back over to the coffee table, to the matchstick delivery I've been staring at just as long as he's been staring at the wall.

The package means only one thing. Isolde Thorn lit the fire. Whether it was with her own hand or with the hand of another, it doesn't matter. My mother's face flashes in my mind, and my body balks against my brain to push it away, but I can't. All my strength melted onto the floor hours ago.

"Gwen, I want to show you The Shelter we've started in the slums," my mother's voice whispers into my ears. And there she is in my mind, with long dark hair like mine, woven into a braid that dangles down her back. She peers at me with deep green eyes and smiles a lopsided smile. She's human, but she's stronger than any angel I've ever met.

She wasn't a fan of Towton City, and she told my dad as often as she could. When yet another human died in the Coils, she decided to do something about it. In the real way, in the right way. The way that should have worked but didn't because the world is a hellhole, especially this city.

Kole's parents worked with my mom to set up a hidden shelter, a safe place where the humans could find help when they decided they didn't want to give any more blood. She gave them beds, and a clean, safe place to sleep. Food, water, medicine. Mom would sit by their sides and hold their hands, promising to stand by their sides when the vampires next came for them.

Mom tried to save lives. And Isolde Thorn decided it had to stop.

I was there when it happened.

"Mom, a boy in the streets said we should leave." I look up at her. She towers over me, and her long braid barely reaches my fingertips. "Something bad is going to happen."

"What boy?" Her eyes widen the way they do when she's not happy about something.

"I don't know his name." I turn to the row of people and frown. "He said the humans need to leave, too."

"Okay, Gwen honey." She leans down and smooths my hair away from my face. And then before I know it, she picks me up, even though she hasn't done that in years. "Sam, Lydia, we have to go. It's finally happening."

I don't know what it *is or why it's finally happening, but my head feels full of heartbeat sounds. Clutching at my mom's soft shirt, I stay frozen as she orders all the humans out of the beds. They look as scared and confused as I am.*

"Mom, can you call Dad?"

"Not right now, honey, but we'll be home to him soon."

Two vampires as big as elephants move into the doorway of the hidden room. I've never seen them before, but they look a lot like the other vampires who sneak around the slums a lot. My mom always tells me to stay away from them because they're part of a bad gang called the Blackthorns.

"Shit, the kid's here," one of them says.

Mom squeezes me tighter against her chest and turns so that I'm facing away from the vampires in the doorway. "Please don't hurt my daughter. Please."

One of the vampires clears his throat. "Put her down, and we'll let her go."

My mom begins to shake. She lowers me to the ground, but I cling onto her waist. I won't let her go. I won't. One of the vampires grabs me. I shriek and kick and flail my arms, but he holds onto me too tight for me to go back to her side.

"Do it," he says to the other one.

"Mommy!" I scream, and the gun goes off loud. Shot after shot after shot. Tears run into my mouth, and I clap my hands over my ears to stop the noise.

I scream. And scream. And scream.

At some point, the vampires leave. And then at another point, someone takes me out of that place and cleans the blood from my hands from where they'd been patting my mom's face. I think it's my dad. It doesn't matter though. I see red for days.

"GWEN, I'm going to do it." Kole's gravelly voice knocks me out of my reverie. The matchstick plummets to the floor as I twist to face him.

"You're going to do what?" I ask.

He blinks, frowns, and meets my gaze. "I'm going to give Isolde Thorn her market."

"What?" My voice cracks, and I slide across the floor to take his face in my hands. "You can't."

"Yes, I can." He points at the matchstick with a shaky finger. "You saw the note. If we don't do what she wants, she'll kill Elliott. I can't let her do that."

"But if we give it back, she gets away with it all. She wins."

My brain can't grasp why Kole would want to give Isolde Thorn back her market, especially after what she's done. It would mean we lose any small victory that we have over her.

"She's already won," Kole says. "I won't let her hurt us any more than she already has."

He stands and leaves the living room without another glance my way. I push up from the floor and follow, but my socked feet drag against the hardwood floor. Kole is just hurt. I understand how he feels. I don't want to argue when he's like this, but I also can't let the one step forward we've taken be undone by grief.

"Kole, I can't let you do this," I say.

"You can't stop me." He pushes the elevator button. "You don't even understand how to use the program."

I cross my arms and slip between Kole and the elevator doors. "I saw enough that I'm pretty sure I could figure it out. If you unlock the market, I'll just lock it again."

"I'll change the password. You won't be able to get in." Kole's glazed eyes don't even look at me. They just stare past at the elevator doors sliding open with a soft whir.

"You can't be serious," I say.

"If it wasn't for you and Silas Thorn, this never would have happened. Now move out of my way."

My head jerks as if I've been slapped. "Kole."

"Just stop. It's over, Gwen. All of this is over. She won. If you keep going after her and she kills Elliott, too, then I'll never speak to you again."

"You can't mean that."

"It's her life, Gwen. I won't risk her like this."

There's nothing more to say. Kole has taken all my words, crunched them up into ragged balls, and tossed them into the trash. So, instead of standing in his way, I trail after him as he shuffles into my father's office, logs into the program, and unlocks the Blood Market. The entire time, my mom's face flickers in my mind. I always thought the memory would overwhelm me with grief and pain when I opened myself to it. But instead, all I feel is nothing. Numb and empty and powerless to stop a thing.

Kole is right. Isolde Thorn won, but she won a long time ago.

CHAPTER 25
SILAS

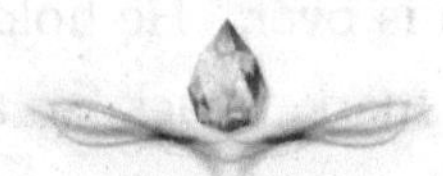

Face smashed against the ground, I roll over and pry open my eyes. At some point during Craig's physical barrage, the world sucked away all evidence of light. I must have passed out, though how much time has ticked by since then is impossible to tell inside this warehouse. No windows, no sunlight, no clock.

Through swollen eyes, I peer through the cell's thick bars. Craig is gone, and I'm alone. He must be satisfied by my lack of answers because he never would have stopped otherwise. As I push onto my elbows, my entire body winces as a hammer slams into my skull. At least I had some blood. I'll heal soon enough.

With a groan, I stare up at the blinding fluorescent lights. Craig did this to me. The one person my mother recruited who ever showed a sliver of humanity. My fingers find my pockets and then the sharp-edged army toys inside. If he did this to me, there's nothing to stop me from retaliating with worse.

The echo of a slamming door reverberates throughout the warehouse and ricochets against my eardrums. I squint toward the clack of shoes on the concrete-slabbed floor. Craig walks into my line of vision, and the salty scent of fried food wafts into the cell. He nods when he sees me and lifts up a brown bag of fast food.

"Silas, I see you're awake," he says in a gruff voice.

"I didn't realize torture came with a side order of french fries."

"The messy business is over." He holds the food through the bars. "The Boss has her market back, so all is well and everyone is happy."

"You might want to rethink your definition of everyone."

"It could be worse." He shakes the bag, and the greasy food rustles inside. "You'll be treated well from now on. Come on, I know you like to eat food."

I don't dignify that with an answer. Instead, I close my eyes and groan.

Craig grunts, unlocks the cell, and comes to kneel beside me. He sets down the food and prods my face with rough hands. "Stop being dramatic. It's only a few bruises."

I know, I think. My hands soar out from my pockets and slam the sharp pieces into the sides of Craig's neck. The plastic barely slips beneath his skin, but it's enough. He jerks and falls to the ground just as I launch up and throw a kick at his face. My boot connects with his teeth and blood hurtles through the air.

He snatches the machine gun. The sleek barrel stares me in the face. Craig releases the safety and slides his finger into the trigger as I stand rooted to the spot.

"You wouldn't," I hiss at him.

"Oh, I would." When he smiles, red stains every inch of his teeth. "In fact, I'd enjoy it."

"What has she done to you to make you this way?" I shake

my head. “I remember when you saved innocents instead of attacking them.”

He spits blood at my feet. “You’re not innocent. Not even close. I know what you’ve done under your assassin name, and you’re just as bad as I am. You’re one of us, Silas, whether you admit it to yourself or not.”

“I am not one of you.” My face throbs from the multitude of bruises, and I dig my teeth into my tongue to distract my mind from the pain. I refuse to show weakness before someone accusing me of being just another worm amidst a nest of thousands.

“Maybe not. Because from what I’ve heard, you feel no remorse.” Craig edges slowly off the ground while keeping the gun pointed at my face. “At least my conscience keeps me company after the things I do. One day I’ll pay my debts, but it won’t be today, and it won’t be to let a serial murderer escape.”

A serial murderer. I suck in a sharp breath and take a step back. His hard glinting eyes follow me as if he’s watching a shark, his finger held tight against the trigger. Craig means every word. I was wrong. He’s different with me not because he’s changed, though he has, but because he believes I’m a monster just like him, just like everyone else that surrounds him. He agrees with Gwen.

“You’re twisting the truth about what I do.” I take another step toward the open cage doors.

He chuckles and mimics my step. “Your concept of reality is what’s twisted. You go out into the streets every night to hunt. You follow a pattern. That’s the definition of a serial killer.”

I can’t listen to this. I can’t let him put doubts into my mind. Everything he’s saying is right, but it’s not as black and white as his words make it out to be. He can’t be right. Can he? Gwen’s angry face flashes in my mind. My mate thinks I'm a monster, too. Everyone does.

"There's more to it than that," I finally say.

"Keep telling yourself that, Silas."

He takes a step forward, and I take a step back. His finger twitches against the trigger, and a smile lifts his lips. He shoves the barrel of the gun into my stomach faster than I can blink. The world freezes.

"Move back to the corner of the cell, Silas."

I do as I'm told, anger pulsing off my body in waves.

Craig leaves me backed against the bars as he slides the cell door shut and twists the lock. "You made a big mistake. Now I'm going to have to tell the Boss what you've done."

MOMENTS EKE by in slow-motion until Craig returns to the warehouse, my mother click-clacking just behind. I thought her face would be all scowls and wrinkles, but a sickly sweet expression curls across her features instead. When she reaches the cell, she looks me up and down while clucking her tongue.

"I gave you a chance to prove you wouldn't cause any trouble." Her eyes flick to the toys scattered around the cell. "And just as I expected, you couldn't even go a day without attacking someone."

"Let me guess," I say as I hover in the middle of the cage. "These toys were part of some sort of test to see if I'd use them against Craig. Just another one of your deranged experiments."

"I assumed you'd go for the Mouse Trap pieces."

"Rookie mistake. If you decided to check the box, you could easily tell if I'd taken a piece."

"Always so clever." Her false smile twists into a frown. "You do understand that we can no longer accommodate you in such a luxurious way."

I nod at the concrete floor. "This is luxurious?"

"I've given you a clean and warm little room with a bed, some entertainment, and a guard willing to get you fresh meals and blood." She gives Craig a pointed look as he swipes the blood from his chin. "You have now attacked him, and I can no longer waste the time and manpower to keep watch over you."

My eyes flick to Craig's tight grip on his gun. "This sounds like what you say when you're ready to dispose of someone."

"Don't be overly dramatic, Silas." She claps her hands. Several more Nightshade vampires filter into the warehouse, all armed as heavily as Craig. "We're moving you to the Coils. I believe you've met your new guard. He's one of my weapons providers, and you gave him quite the scare when you took your little sniper rifle."

"You can't be serious." My mind turns back to my trip into the Coils for the weapon, to the man meant to hang the orange rag warning me if my mother began to infiltrate the slums. And yet, she's gotten to him first, just like always.

"Just one more question," I ask before she goes. "How did you manage it anyway? The Nicky Tanner I killed was a vampire."

My mother laughs. "I found a new creature out in No Man's Land and an amulet that could control it. A vuulectian, a shapeshifter. I was able to force its form to shift from a vampire into an angel, even after its death. It's unfortunate I had to sacrifice it that way. Perhaps I can find a few others to take its place. They are so useful, after all."

I shake my head. Of course. It was the only thing that made sense. I should have seen it days ago. Nicky Tanner never was an angel *or* a vampire. We'd all been played.

Craig unlocks the cage and strides over to my side. There are no joking comments, no slight smiles from him this time. His face is hard and set in stone as he points the barrel of the gun at my forehead. I lift my chin and look straight into the scope.

"To keep you from doing anything stupid, you won't be going awake." He twists the gun around and slams the butt into my skull. The world becomes shadows.

CHAPTER 26
GWEN

The night after my fight with Kole, I box up my boots and shove them under my bed, retiring my night job before it even really begins. After that, the days pass in a blur, the way the world slides by when I rev my bike down the city streets. Kole barely speaks to me now, and Elliott shoots me frantic looks when I see her at work, pushing her pearls around as if I set fire to her house myself.

Towton City goes to hell. The *24/7 News* highlights a full-blown war between the vampires gangs, complete with a running death count ticking in the righthand corner of the screen. Both sides take casualties, but Isolde Thorn has an easy lead, since Bobby Shade is no longer in the picture.

The only good thing is, the Saints cancel the execution. They saw Silas's confession, and they decide to let my father go.

When he walks through my apartment's front door, his face is slack and drawn as if he's been hidden away from the sun for years, not days. His face is still the best sight I've seen in years, though. I jump into his arms, burying my face in his neck. He squeezes me so tight, my lungs can't find air, but I don't care. He's here. He's fine. They let him go.

I sit him down on the stool in my kitchen and whip up some pancakes for breakfast. He's going to need a lot of food and lot of sleep and—

"Gwen," he says, his voice eerily calm. "We need to talk about Isolde Thorn. I heard she's back in town. And that she's abducted Orpheus."

I've tried not to think about Silas since his abduction, and I certainly haven't talked to anyone else about him until now. The not-thinking thing hasn't totally worked. My mind wars with itself every single day. He lied to me for so long. My father could have been executed by his not coming clean. But there are still so many questions surrounding it all. And I can't help but worry if he's all right.

"You heard right." I spoon a pancake onto a plate and put it before him, but he ignores the food.

He leans toward me, his eyes flashing with anger. "Tell me everything that's happened. Now."

My father doesn't say a word as I explain it all. It takes me a good twenty minutes to get through the full story, starting with my initial run-in with Orpheus to the day I found out he killed Nicky Tanner. Dad's eyes grow harder with my every word.

"I saw him kill Nicky Tanner," he finally says. "And he wasn't lying to you. That supernatural was a vampire, someone stalking a girl. Looked like the vamp planned on killing her."

All the blood drains from my face. "Wait, what?"

"I saw it happen, Gwen."

I fall silent, my mind racing. If my father saw Silas kill the vampire, he could have easily told the Saints, and maybe he wouldn't have spent an entire week trapped in their dungeon. He had the ability to save himself, but instead he just sat there, waiting for his execution.

"I don't understand," I whisper. "You could have told them he did it."

"It wouldn't have changed a thing," he says. "I saw him kill a *vampire*. They found an angel's body in the exact same place, wearing the same clothes, using the same name. It doesn't make any sense, and they would have said I was making things up to get myself out of there."

I sit hard on a stool. "So, he didn't kill an angel."

"No, he did not."

I shake my head. "He still lied to me, though."

Dad sighs and gives me a sad smile. "Maybe he was in the wrong, and maybe he lied to you about it, but he is trying to do the right thing, Gwen. It sounds like he was trying to help you find another way to get me out of there. It's a shame none of it worked. If the Saints get their hands on him now, he'll be dead. And this city is worse without him patrolling the streets."

"I thought you didn't approve of killing, even vampires who hunt."

"He kills to save lives."

"But." I shake my head. "What about your code?"

"I'm not as noble as you think, Gwen. The only thing that has stopped me all these years are thoughts of your mother. Olivia would have wanted me to show mercy. She would have wanted me to show compassion, even to the worst of them." He leans forward and drops his voice to a whisper. "Towton City needs him. He's willing to do what I'm not. And you shouldn't hold yourself back, either."

This is the most my dad has said to me since Mom died. It took the threat of execution, some dungeon bars, and angry angels for the walls to crumble between us. And now that he's *really* speaking to me, he's saying what I never imagined he'd say. All this time I thought he trained me only because I pestered him to do so, and that he never wanted me to fight back myself. But now I see my ambitions are not just my own. My dad wants me to help this city, too.

"All right," I say with a nod. "So, what's the plan?"

He smiles. "The plan is, you'll stay here while I go hunt down Isolde Thorn. It's time I kick her out of town again."

"If you think I'm staying here, the dungeons got to your head more than I thought they would. Besides, you need to rest. Eat your pancakes."

"People are dying. They can't wait for me to eat pancakes."

For fuck's sake. I should have known he'd say that. He's been free for less than half an hour, and already he's planning his next mission.

"Well, then I'm coming with you. You need my help."

He folds his arms and gives me a once-over. "I see my absence has made you more confident."

"Because I'm a damn good fighter."

"You're not bad." He nods. "Go change, and we'll do this together."

Before he can change his mind, I jog to my room, grab my boots from beneath my bed, and change into my fighting gear. This is it. The moment we take down the Blackthorns, end the gang war, and free the humans from the Coils.

And when we find Isolde, we'll find Silas, too. I have to hope he's okay.

When I stride back into the kitchen, the stool is empty and cool air rushes in from an open window. I cross the room and stare out at the streets below. He left. On his wings, no doubt, which means I'll never be able to catch up to him.

He's going to take down the Blackthorns without me.

AS THE MOON sinks into the river, I stand on the wooden dock watching the boat bob along to a lapping river soundtrack. The sliding door is scattered in a million tiny shards on the boat's whitewashed deck, and the recent winter storms have snatched papers from inside and strewn them all around the Boat Basin. Several pairs of muddy footprints lead from right where I'm standing, into the boat, and back out again. Either some squatters have taken up residence or I'm not the first person to check out this place.

If I was a betting kind of girl, I'd go with the latter.

Since my father decided to find Isolde on his own, I'm on the hunt for Orpheus, just in case he's trapped somewhere else. His house seemed the best place to start, though truth be told, I don't have a shred of hope in finding him here.

Fisting my hands, I slowly ease onto the deck and poke my head through the smashed doorway. Inside, everything sits just how it did the last time I was here. Plain black furniture. Plain walls without adornment. Even the hit list is gone. Someone has been here to rip apart Silas's maps and photos, leaving behind nothing but a tornado of scraps.

"Are you looking for Silas?" a woman's voice sounds from behind me.

I jump and whirl towards the voice, clenched hands raised as high as my chin. The frazzle-haired woman widens red-streaked eyes and backs away, her slippered feet crunching a pile of broken glass.

"I'm sorry." I drop my hands to my sides. "I was worried you'd be someone else."

She nods and pats at her hair as a gray strand falls into her eyes. "It's okay, dear. Things haven't been as calm around here since poor Silas was taken. I know he's Orpheus, you know."

"What do you mean?" Maybe this woman can give me some insight into what happened here, though I have a sneaking suspicion only Isolde Thorn could have done this.

"That mother of his." She licks her lips and glances over her shoulder as if she expects Isolde Thorn to pop out of the shadows at any moment. I don't blame her. "She came around here not long after Silas got taken and had one of her Soldiers smash down the doors. That vampire is bad news. I wouldn't be surprised if she took Silas herself."

"Did you tell anyone?" I ask.

"I didn't have anyone to tell, I'm afraid. Until now."

I nod. If Isolde has been here, she must have seen Silas's maps and photos. Now all of the information he gathered over the years is in her head. That can't be a good thing.

"Don't worry," I tell her. "I'm convinced she took Silas, and I'm going to get him back."

The woman before me smiles as if I've presented her with a year's worth of cake. "Good girl. He needs someone like you."

I shift on my feet and flick my gaze to the glass-covered ground. If only she knew I sat on this decision for days. And only hours earlier, I still assumed the worst. I'm probably the last person Silas wants to break him free from his prison.

"Did you see or hear anything that could help?" I ask instead of responding to her comment.

"Hmm." She nibbles at her bottom lip and scrunches up her nose, making her seem more like a ten-year-old than someone's grandmother. "I sure did. That mother of his said something about a warehouse."

"A warehouse? Do you know where?"

She shakes her head and frowns. "I'm sorry, dear. She was

shouting at one of those Soldiers of hers about getting back to the warehouse, but that's all she said."

"That's okay. It's still something to go on. There aren't that many warehouses in Towton City."

She wraps her cotton throw tighter around her shivering shoulders. "If you find him, tell him that cat of his is okay. I came right over here as soon as I saw the news and took her over to my boat. She's hardly even limping anymore. He'll be glad to hear that, so you tell him, okay?"

I smile. "I'll tell him."

"You know, I really did think there was something different about him." She smiles back. "And I was right, you see."

"What do you mean?"

"The last time he came over to my boat, he wasn't his grumpy self. He made cookies for me, you see. Silas is always so helpful, but he carries the weight of the world on his shoulders. I blame that mother, and the way she treated him. But that day…" She glances up at the darkening sky, and a full-faced smile beams across her features. "That day he didn't seem like that at all. You've made him lighter."

My heart trembles inside my chest, and I shake my head. I don't make Silas feel lighter. If anything, I've made his world ten times heavier just by being in it. "I really doubt that has anything to do with me. Maybe he just likes baking cookies."

"Maybe." She squeezes my arm, but her smile doesn't dim. "You be careful now…what was your name, dear?"

"Gwen," I say. "Gwen Kane."

"Oh." She squeezes my arm even tighter and lowers her voice to a whisper. She even winks. "I know who you are. Phantom's daughter. You've been fighting the gangs out there. No wonder he likes you."

"I was fighting," I reply. "But…"

Her hand tightens on my arm. "We need someone like you, Gwen Kane. We have so many humans here, and the Houses will never have us. The city can't go on like this. You need to do something. For the Houseless."

I stare at her for a good long while before answering while an idea begins to form in my mind. "Well then. Maybe we'll form our own fucking House. And every human in this city will be welcome."

CHAPTER 27
SILAS

"You need to wake up now. We have an important visitor coming." Larry, my captor, blows rancid breath onto my face.

I pry open my eyes and stare up at him through a hazy cloud. My miniature cage sits in the corner of his dilapidated weapons room on top of a pile of dried mud, and I have to put my knees to my chest just to fit inside. Every muscle in my body aches. It's been days since I've had any blood.

"What time is it?" I ask in a voice that scrapes like a shovel against ice.

He pokes a long, skinny finger through the bars. "It's almost seven at night. You've been sleeping all day. But someone's coming, and you need to get up."

There's only one window in this stuffy room, and it opens out onto the slum walkways, which are always full of shadows. Ever since my mother moved me into this hellhole, day has turned to night and night has turned to day. Sleep has become my one and only past-time other than thinking up ways in which to destroy the man who pokes and prods at me every hour of every day.

"Exciting," I say. "Who do you have coming over this time?"

He smiles, showing me a mouthful of chipped teeth, and rubs his hands together. "The Boss lady is coming."

I roll my eyes. "Fucking yay."

"She's picking up some weapons." He laughs. "She also wants to ask you some questions, so you need to be up and at 'em."

I spread open my arms, and my hands hit either side of the cage. "This is about as up and at 'em as I'm going to get. Unless you let me out."

He waves his finger back and forth as if it's a ticking clock. "Uh uh. Stop trying to trick me into letting you out. I'm not stupid. You'll rip my throat out to get at my blood."

"So you say." I take a swig from the water bottle in my cell. There are a few drops left, and the lukewarm water slips down my scratchy throat. It doesn't do a damn thing to stop the ache in my canines. If Larry isn't careful, I'll go into a blood rage.

"Before I forget." Larry smiles and digs an orange cloth from his baggy jeans pocket. He slips the end through my cell bars and ties the cloth in a knot. "I told you I'd warn you when she came around here, so there you go."

I narrow my eyes and stare him down. He licks his lips. The second I step outside of this cell, the second Larry's dead. And he knows it. Antagonizing me is the wrong move. As soon as I get my chance, I'll show him the true monster, the one everyone believes is inside me.

A loud knock makes Larry pop up and poke an eye at the view. His shoulders relax, but his fingers still twitch at his sides. When he opens the door, he reveals my mother in a perfectly-pressed white suit and matching heels. She must get a whiff of Larry's den because her nose bunches up.

"Hello, Boss lady," he says. "Come on in."

She takes a small step inside with Craig just behind her. As soon as the door slams shut, her eyes find me in my tiny corner cell. Frowning, she whispers something to Craig before turning her focus to my current guard.

"Larry, when you receive your next payment, you should hire a cleaner to bleach this place. It's smelling a little...stale," she says. "I can't have one of my own living in this kind of squalor. It doesn't make me look very good."

"Yes, Boss lady." He ruffles a hand on his beard.

"Also, when was the last time you let him out for a shower or a bath?" She raises her eyebrows at me, and for the first time, she shows concern over my current predicament. That can only mean I have something she wants, and whatever it is, I'd prefer to stay right fucking here.

"Well, I never have, Boss lady. I can't let him out of there..." He swallows hard. "He'd only attack me."

She clucks her tongue against the roof of her mouth. "If you want to become one of my Soldiers, you need to show less fear in front of a vampire you have caged up in the corner."

"Yes, Boss lady."

"Now." My mother frowns at me from across the room. She won't step further inside, lest the filth stain her white as snow suit. "Silas, I need to ask you a few questions. Are you going to cooperate this time?"

"I don't see why I should."

My mother continues on as if I haven't said a thing. "The darling Elliott Edwards has given me some enlightening information. Is it true Gwen Kane has an enormous stash of valuables inside her apartment building? Lots of angel feathers and shifter blood?"

My face stays exactly as it is, but inside, my mind races. If she's telling the truth, my mother has gotten to Elliott. But in what sense? Either she's turned her to the Blackthorn side or she's trapped her just like me. Both options can only spell trouble. "As I keep telling you, Gwen Kane hates me. She doesn't confide in me."

"That's just as well." She smiles. "I just wanted to double check Elliott's story. She claims not to know the code to get into the room with the valuables."

"Of course she doesn't." I shrug, though the full movement is stopped short by the cramped space. "She doesn't live there."

"But Gwen does know the code to the room."

I frown. "Unlikely."

Her smile widens. "You're lying. I can always tell, Silas."

Fuck.

I choke out a harsh laugh. "What exactly is your plan? You're going to steal some vials of vampire saliva?"

"Exactly." She spreads her hands out in front of her as if this is the most sensible plan in the world. To her, it probably is. More resources equals more power in Isolde Thorn's mind, and if her opposition has none at all, then she's the only one left controlling everything.

"You're wrong. Gwen doesn't have a code to anything."

"Even if she doesn't, Kole Mason might."

Dammit. If my mother goes after Kole, Gwen would take that harder than if my mother went after Gwen herself. "Kole doesn't know a damn thing. He lives on the top floor of the building, and he doesn't get involved with Phantom's things."

"Uh uh. That was another lie." She wags a finger at me. "It's a shame, really. All you have to do is cooperate, and I'll move you out of this…stink hole."

Larry pops over to her side. "No, please, Boss lady. I'm taking good care of him."

She sniffs. "Craig, can you please call my second-in-command and have him set up a meeting with Miss Edwards? Be sure to schedule it after your warehouse sweep so you can join us as well."

"You have a new second?" I ask, and then I curse myself for showing even a hint of interest.

"Well, yes. As my old one vanished after I left the city, I needed to fill his shoes, didn't I?"

"But it took you years to pick the last one," I say.

"This one has already proven himself more than capable, though he's merely my acting second-in-command for now. If you would only cooperate, I could keep the business inside the family, you know. You could be my second."

"Never."

She rolls her eyes and snaps her fingers at Larry. "I need a new gun for my second, please. With a silencer. After I drain Phantom's stash, we'll have some loose ends to tie up, so to speak."

"If you touch a single hair on Gwen's head, I will—"

She cuts a sharp glance my way. "I only meant Kole and Elliott, but if you don't stop threatening me, I'll add your mate's name to my list." She smiles when my eyes widen. "Yes, that's right, Silas. I've figured a few things out. I know what Gwen is to you. And I will not hesitate to use her to make a point."

Red snakes into my vision. I grip the metal bars in my dry hands and shake them with all my might. My mother only gives me the slightest of glances before taking the weapon from

Larry's hands. She's going after Kole and Elliott, and when they're done giving her exactly what she needs, she'll dispose of them.

And then, she'll go after my mate.

CHAPTER 28
GWEN

Back in the office, I stare down at an in-depth Towton City map I printed off the computer. It's a year old, but it shows every single building in the city, numbered and cross-referenced with a pamphlet that details the build date and the owner.

Our building is listed as being under private ownership, which is what I figure Isolde Thorn's warehouses will list. There can't be many privately owned warehouses in Towton City, so I'll stake out each one until I find Silas. After that, I'll fight my way inside and get him out of there, and hopefully catch up to whatever my father is doing.

Two hours later, I have my short list. Three warehouses down by the docks, and a cluster of new builds up near Diamond Bay. My gut says Uptown makes the most sense because Isolde would never trek into enemy territory unless absolutely necessary.

Just as I'm about to leave, a soft knock sounds by the door. Kole stands inside the office with a deep-set frown twisting his face.

"Why are you in your fighting gear?" he asks.

I sigh and let my hands drop to my sides. I knew this conversation needed to happen eventually, but I'd hoped it would happen *after* tonight, not now. "I have to do something, Kole."

"You're going to go after her, aren't you?" His shoulders shake as he digs his fingers into the doorframe. "Even after what happened to Eric and what will happen to Elliott. You just can't help yourself."

"She needs to be stopped," I say.

"Then let someone else deal with it!" His booming voice makes my bones jump out of my skin. Face full of harsh lines and eyes clouded by furrowed brows, Kole barely looks like my best friend anymore.

"I did." I raise my hands to my sides, the volume of my voice rising along with them. "Dad left a few hours ago, and he hasn't come back yet. He needs my help. Silas needs my help."

"I meant what I said." His jaw muscles ripple like a churning sea. "I'll never speak to you again."

Tears sneak out of my eyes and slip down my cheeks. My only hope is that one day Kole will understand why I had to do this. One day, maybe he can forgive me for not being the sister he needs. "I know."

"Fine. When you get back, I'll be gone."

"No." Heart leaping into my throat, I take a step toward him. "Kole, please don't do this."

"I'll go stay with Elliott to make sure she's safe," he says. "In her new apartment, the one she got since her old one *burned down*."

He turns and walks away from me, and a moment later, the slamming door rockets against my eardrums. An emptiness settles inside my chest, and I force myself to blink it away. I take a long, deep breath and wipe the tears from my cheeks before shifting focus to the map.

"You can do this," I whisper.

WHEN I REACH MY DESTINATION, I wait in the shadows. No movement or sound echoes from the bank of warehouses near Diamond Bay, but a lone car sits near the entrance to the one at the very end. I take a deep breath and stride across the empty parking lot, my boots crunching the thick gravel.

When I reach the garage door, I drop to my knees and peer under the open sliver. Inside, rows upon rows of blood bags cover the tables. Shoes clack near my face, and the door clatters up. My body wars between fight or flight, but my mind weighs in just in time to send me into fight stance mode. I jump up from the ground and bend my legs, raising my fists before me.

Quick scan of attacker: male, shaped like a tank, a massive gun slung under his arm, and a face that rings a familiar bell in my brain. He's Craig Martinez, and he stole Silas from the streets.

His eyes widen when they land on me. Fingers reaching for his gun, he glances away just long enough for me to take aim. My boot soars out and slams into the gun. Slipping from his shoulder, the weapon skitters across the ground. Craig Martinez blinks. I blink. Heart galloping at record speed, I jog sideways and kick the gun further away. If he wants to take me down, he'll have to do it the fair way. With a smile, I roll back my shoulders and raise my fists to my chin.

He holds up his hands and shakes his head. "Okay, stop. What do you want?"

"Is Silas inside?" I ask.

"Nope." He takes a crunching step sideways toward the gun. "We moved him days ago."

"What about my father?"

"He's not here, either.

I narrow my eyes and match his step. "Where are they?"

"I'm not going to tell you that."

"Well, then I'll make you tell me." I edge sideways to block his progress toward the gun, fists raised and body braced for attack. This vampire is about three times my size, but I'm quick on my feet, and I'm pretty fucking motivated right now.

He sighs and shoves his hands into his pockets, rocking back on his heels. "I'm not going to get into a fist fight with a half-human woman."

"Oh yeah?" My lips spread into a smile. I love it when people underestimate me. "Then, you better tell me where Silas and my father are."

"You know what? Fine. Silas was taken into the slums a couple days ago. He's being guarded by a human named Larry. And your father? No clue. Haven't seen him."

So, Dad didn't come here. Then, where the hell is he?

"Where inside the slums?" I ask.

"Fourth level, left-most tunnel. Has a dragon on the door. You can't miss it."

"All right." I jog a few steps back and snatch the gun from the ground, all without taking my eyes off his boxy figure. "Why would you tell me all this?"

"Because I'm going to call the Boss as soon as you leave, and then you'll have to deal with *her* instead of me. She won't have any problems hitting you." He crosses his arms and smirks as if he's somehow won this encounter, even though I'm the one with the machine gun.

Frowning, I lift the gun and aim it at his stomach. "Hand over your phone."

He shakes his head. "I know who you are. You won't shoot me."

"Oh yeah?" I raise my eyebrows and take a few steps closer. "Maybe not. But I hear the back of these things can really hurt."

Whipping the gun around, I haul back and throw all my strength behind shoving the butt into his forehead, where it hits with a loud *crunch*. His mouth opens, his eyes roll back into his skull, and he tumbles to the ground. With a smile, I slip his phone from his pocket and jog back across the parking lot. But each step becomes heavier as his words sink in. Silas is being held in one place I never want to go. If I'm going to rescue him, I have to go inside the Coils.

MY STOMACH CLENCHES SO tight I feel as if I might vomit at any second. Cables zig-zag overhead, multicolored grime plasters the walls, and water drips down the buildings, forming puddles at my feet. The only light shines from a dangling lightbulb several yards down the twisting maze.

My mother's face flashes in my mind, and I swallow back the thick lump blocking my airwaves. Taking a deep breath, I let the memory wash over me. Red stains the walls, stains my hands, stains her face. A hollow ache takes residence inside my chest, but unlike before, I don't push it away. If I try to bottle it up, the hysteria swirling around my stomach might take root and send me hyperventilating to my knees.

Closing my eyes, I force myself to focus. Deep breath in, deep breath out. Deep breath in, deep breath out. Finally, I crack open my eyes, and even though my stomach still churns, the nausea doesn't consume me.

Come on, Gwen. You can do this.

Something scuttles nearby, and my entire body jumps out of its skin. I step into the shadows and press my back against the wet wall. A vampire in a top hat shuffles by, and his eyes widen when they sweep across me. He grins and rockets toward me as quick as a rat on steroids. I shouldn't have tossed Craig Martinez's machine gun.

Quick scan of attacker: the Mad Hatter. Enough said.

I jump out and throw my left hook. As my fist smashes into his stomach, I launch an uppercut into his jaw. He shrieks and smacks my face hard with the back of his hand. Pain explodes in my jaw, and I stumble back to blink out the stars. He rushes at me, wraps his arms around my waist, and slams me into the wall.

I scream and twist like a snake in his arms. Shoving at his chest, I punch his chin so hard I must rattle the teeth in his skull. He growls and lets go, and as he backs away, he whips his head back and forth as if he's trying to shake something free.

I wait, steadying my ragged breath. *Get it together, Gwen.* The Mad Hatter licks his lips, flashing his canines. I brace myself and bend my knees. Narrowing my eyes, I smile. That's all it takes. He rushes toward me, and I swing my leg up at his face. He catches my shin, just like Dad, but this time I know it's coming. I use his weight to throttle him to the ground.

Sucking a breath, I yank my leg from his grip and hurtle it into his back. He falls, and his elbows slam into the ground. Frantic fingers grasp for the gun at his back, but I rip it from his pants and point it at his head.

"Probably not a good idea to move." My hands shake from the hot adrenaline that rushes through me.

"You know, you're almost as pesky as Orpheus," he says in a singsong voice.

"What are you doing in here?" I demand.

"Looking for Blain Shade. The traitor."

"Blain?" I frown. "What are you talking about?"

"Blain Shade." He laughs and rolls over to stare up at me with a demented smile. "That asshole has been playing us all. Even poor Layla Pirelli."

I freeze and slide my finger over the safety of the gun but find it's already off. Instead, I press my thumb on the hammer, the *click* almost as loud as a gunshot. I have no idea if that actually does anything useful, but it sounds threatening enough.

"Explain," I say.

"He framed Phantom to get on Isolde Thorn's good side, using poor little Layla. Apparently, she was even going to leave Vincent for him. And now he's Isolde's second-in-command. Can you believe it?"

"You're making this up," I say, taking slow steps backward down the tunnel and away from the Mad Hatter. "Isolde Thorn wouldn't work with someone related to Bobby Shade. Plus, he's never wanted to be involved."

"You're wrong."

I shake my head. Blain Shade can't be the one pulling the strings. He always kept himself separated from his family's business.

But, a little voice says in my mind, *it does make sense.* Someone close to the Nightshade gang was always involved. Someone Layla would trust. If they were *involved,* then of course she'd keep his identity a secret, and it would explain why she and Vincent were seen fighting just before Silas and I approached her.

It could have been him that night outside Vincent's place,

too. His body fits the build, and the voice could be a match. That's why he let me go. He *knows* me.

But why would he do this?

The Mad Hatter pops up from the ground and races toward me, his feet splashing in sewage. His eyes harden, and a broken grin splits his lips. Gritting my teeth, I tighten my hands around the gun and aim. My finger twitches at the trigger. It pulls. The force slams against my body, and I stumble back, throwing a hand over my mouth at what I've done.

No! But I can't take it back. The bullet slams into the Mad Hatter's right knee. Blood explodes through his pants, and he falls to the ground with a howl. Heart racing, I twist on my heels and run.

CHAPTER 29
SILAS

"Stop pacing," I say. "And just let me out."

Larry's frown wrinkles his entire face. "If I do let you have a shower like the Boss lady wants, will you cooperate?"

"I'll be on my best behavior," I say with a twisted smile. And by best behavior, I mean I will rip apart his spindly little neck in my hands. The longer he stalls, the worse it will be. I need to get Uptown and warn Gwen, even though I am likely the last person she wants to see.

A thump sounds from the door, and I swallow back a groan. Another visitor will only delay this process. Larry presses his eye against the view and stands there for several moments before stepping back with a frown. His hands twitch at his sides. A second *thump*. Larry's shoulders lurch like a bucking horse.

"Are you going to answer that?"

"I can't see no one," he says in a whisper. He clears his throat and raises his voice. "Who's there?"

Silence stretches out the moments. Then, *thump, thump*.

How interesting. I shift around inside my cage until I have a better view of the door. Larry paces back and forth, and his bare feet flop against the wood.

"What do you reckon?" He snatches the closest weapon, a small hand gun he probably can't even use properly. An expert in military weaponry, perhaps, but when it comes to the more practical pistols, Larry doesn't even bother to turn off the safety.

If I were him, I would never open the door, but I'm not Larry. Thank the universe for that. Whoever is playing games out there may only spell trouble for me as well, but on the other hand, they could spell freedom in big glorious letters. Anyone against Larry would surely unlock this cage and set his prisoner free.

"I would go ahead and see what's there," I say with a smile. "My mother doesn't treat cowards kindly."

Larry clutches his gun and takes small shuffling steps toward the door. He reaches out with twitching fingers, barely skimming the surface of the lock. With a deep breath, he pulls back the bolt and moves a hand toward the knob.

The door blasts open with a loud *crash*. The wood smacks into Larry's head, knocking him to the ground, where the gun clatters away from him. I grip my hands around the thick metallic bars as heavy boots clomp into the room. Gwen fucking Kane steps into Larry's den with bright red lips shining under the cheap lights.

"That's my mate," I practically purr.

"No, no, no." Larry scrabbles back on the floor. "Don't hurt me."

"Where's Silas?" she asks in a harsh tone that means pure business.

"In the corner. He's just in the corner."

Gwen's eyes sail across the room and land on me. Her mouth

drops open, and deep lines spirit across her forehead. She points a pistol at the man on the ground and kicks him with her heavy boot.

"Get him out of there." She pulls back the hammer with a click, making my lips twists up into a smile. "Now!"

"Yes, ma'am," Larry says in a very similar tone to the one he uses with my mother. He crawls across the floor and unlocks the cage. When he pulls open the door, he refuses to meet my eyes.

With slow, painful movements, I crawl out of the cage and stand. Every bone and muscle strains against me, but a soothing relief washes over me. Gwen just stares, her expression masked by the deep black kohl that lines her eyes.

"You're the last person I expected to come for me," I finally say.

"Don't look so grateful. You were taken three days ago."

"Better late than never."

Gwen's shoulders relax, and her blood-red lips lift into a small smile. Even after everything I've done, Gwen is here, smiling at me. If I didn't know better, I might think she's happy to see the slums haven't destroyed me.

"You came inside the slums," I say. "Without passing out."

She lifts her chin. "Damn straight."

I smile, and then it falters. "Gwen, there's something I need to tell you."

"I don't like the sound of that."

"My mother stopped by earlier to question me about the office. Apparently, she's gotten to Elliott, and now she's going after Kole to get access."

"Kole is with Elliott now." Her eyes film over, and her face drains of all color. "He went over to her new apartment."

"Okay." I grab a gun from the table and slide it into the back of my jeans. "This was a few hours ago, so she's probably gotten to him by now and forced him to do what she wants. We should use the back way to get inside your father's office. That way she won't see us coming."

But as I start for the door, a wave of dizziness causes me to stagger to the side.

Gwen takes my arm. "Silas. What's wrong?"

"I haven't had blood in a few days. It's fine. Let's get going."

"Absolutely not," she says with a frown. "You can't fight if you don't have blood. Take some from me."

"Gwen."

"Don't argue with me, Silas. You need some blood." Swallowing, she steps up close to me and angles her head, exposing her neck to me. That delicate, soft neck. "Take some."

"You know I don't do that," I say, my voice scraping from my throat. "And you know why. My blood rage…"

"I trust you," she whispers to me. "I've got you."

My canines ache, and the temptation to follow through burns within me. She's right. If I don't drink at least a little blood, I'll never be able to fight, if it comes to that. I can barely walk out the fucking door.

But I've gone so long without drinking from someone's neck. I can't afford to lose control. I would never risk Gwen's life like this.

"Orpheus," she whispers to me. "You won't hurt me. You know you won't. I'm your mate."

I shudder. She presses up onto her toes until her neck is only an inch from my face. With trembling hands, I grip her waist. And then I lower my face to her skin, and my canines slice into her throat.

Instantly, her sweet blood coats my tongue. Hunger rips

through me, but I force myself to focus on her, on my mate, to keep myself calm.

She arches her back and moans as I drink. The sound makes me wish we were anywhere but here. I'd taste her blood and then fuck her again and again, burying my cock inside of her, making her scream my name so loud the entire city would hear it.

"You taste so good," I murmur before taking another mouthful of her sweet blood. Iron and magic dance on my tongue, and I lick every last drop she can give me. My body fills with energy. Sounds become louder. Smells become stronger. And Gwen's blood, it tastes so much sweeter.

I want more. I want all of it. But I hold myself back when I've had just enough to get me through the rest of this night. She needs to be strong enough to fight, too, and if I take too much, she'll need to rest for hours.

"Are you all right, Gwen?" I ask when I've dragged my mouth away from her neck.

"More than all right." Her eyelids flutter. "That felt surprisingly good. And see? You didn't harm me. I knew you wouldn't."

Footsteps suddenly thunder toward us. The Mad Hatter shuffles inside, his leg drenched in blood. He rushes toward us, vicious eyes locked on Gwen.

I push her behind me.

"Get out of my way, Orpheus," he hisses at me. "She's fucking dead."

I just laugh. "If you think you can threaten my mate, you're more delusional than I thought."

Powered by the fresh blood, I grab his head and snap his neck faster than he can take his next breath. The Hatter falls to the ground. His vacant eyes stare up at me.

Gwen gasps, and I turn to her, bracing myself for her reaction.

"I'm sorry, Gwen. I—"

"Don't apologize." She grabs my face and kisses me hard. When she pulls back, I don't quite know what to say. "We're assassins. Sometimes, this is what we have to do to save ourselves. Now, come on. We need to save the others, too."

CHAPTER 30
GWEN

Silas and I scale the ladder to the office hatch, my miniature flashlight clenched between my front teeth to light the way. All the way here, my mind played the same sad song over and over again. Kole wouldn't be in danger, if not for me. If I'd only stayed in. If I'd only refrained from donning my boots and pushing him away. If I had, he'd be safe. But if I had, nothing would change.

The line in my head between black and white blurs into a meaningless gray blob. I don't know what to do anymore. I don't know which choices are right and which are wrong. All I know is I'd do anything in the world to save Kole Mason's life, even if that means losing my own soul along the way.

We reach the hatch and pause. As soon as we enter the office, Isolde Thorn will know we're here, and I will finally have to meet her face to face. Right now, we have the element of surprise on our side, but it won't last long. Underneath my hood, tucked into the waist of my black leggings, I've hidden the Mad Hatter's gun.

I don't plan on using it, but just having it there makes me feel more ready to face this woman's cruel face.

"Ready?" I ask in a whisper. Because I'm not.

Silas nods. Quickly, I push the hatch open and crawl into darkness. Silas follows and stands by my side, his shoulder brushing against mine. Seconds pass before the bookcase groans and shifts to the side. The cavernous office rolls into view to reveal Kole, very much alive, typing away at the keyboard. My heart launches into my throat until the next image follows. Behind him, Blain Shade stands holding a gun to his head.

"What the hell?" Silas yanks out a pistol.

"Right. I forgot to mention that." I take several steps into the room to get closer to Kole's side. "Apparently, Blain took the lead role in framing my dad. Meet the new second-in-command."

Blain frowns and whips his gun toward us. Silas and I freeze mid-step. The elevator doors whir open, and Isolde Thorn strides into the office, holding a glass of blood with the tips of her bright red fingernails.

My world stutters to a stop, and my breath lodges in my windpipes. Every moment in my life so far has led me to this place. Right here. Right now. To the moment when I look into the eyes of my mom's true killer. Isolde Thorn never pulled the trigger, but she ordered the hit, and she's the only one responsible in my mind. I suck in a deep, rattling breath, narrow my eyes, and sink my teeth into my tongue.

And all she does is smile.

"I wasn't expecting this little reunion, Silas. I see you managed to find a way out of that cage." She clacks her heels over to Kole's side and drops the glass of blood on the desk. "And dear little Gwen Kane. Clever entrance you have with that bookcase. Can I assume it's your fault my Craig hasn't made his appointment with us this evening?"

"Where's Elliott?" I ask through gritted teeth.

"Oh, that girl." She waves her hand in the air like an opera conductor. "Over there."

My eyes scan the room until they land on Elliott, hunched over in the corner. Thick ropes circle her wrists. Her necklace is broken, and the pearls pepper the floor around her. Red-streaked eyes open wide, she stares at me as her shoulders shake. My father is beside her, tied up just as tightly as she is, though his eyes are shut to the world.

I must gasp out loud because the sound echoes all around me.

"I'm so sorry, Gwen," Elliott says through thick gulps of air. "I shouldn't have told her."

My heart throbs. "It's okay. It's not your fault."

"Enough," Isolde says. "Blain, make sure they don't speak again until all these resources are taken out of here, including all these lovely computers and their interesting programs."

"Blain," I say, ignoring Isolde. If I can somehow talk him over to our side, it will be all of us against her. "Why are you doing this? You've said it before yourself. Getting wrapped up in the gangs is the worst thing in the world."

Blain keeps his aim steady. "Wrong. Getting wrapped up in the *Nightshade* gang is the worst thing in the world."

"How is this any better?"

"I'm second-in-command." He shrugs. "One day I'll be Boss. I never had a chance at that in Nightshade."

"Acting second." Isolde Thorn clucks her tongue. "Silas, I would really like you to set aside your ridiculous ideals and become my heir now. As soon as you have proven yourself, you can take your place as my second."

"Never happening." Silas's voice is as sharp as a switchblade.

"All this power could be yours."

"I don't care about power."

"You care about Gwen, though, don't you?" Isolde Thorn clicks toward me, a sharp glint in her ice blue eyes. I push my hood away, and it drops heavily against my back. Bending into fight stance mode, I raise my clenched hands. If she moves any closer, her face will meet my fists. Instead, she stops and slices a sharp fingernail across her throat. "I'll let your mate survive this as long as you stand down and agree to cooperate."

Silas shifts his body in front of mine. Isolde Thorn launches forward and smacks his head so hard, he falls to the ground. The gun slips from his fingers and rockets across the floor until it disappears into the open hatch. It falls into the tunnel's depths with a reverberating *clunk*. Isolde smiles and kicks out a foot, her sharp heel slicing a deep gash into his forehead. Blood oozes from the wound and clings to her shoe, and when she turns to walk away, she leaves a trail of bloody dots in her wake.

Fear churns through my veins. She's knocked him out. I didn't give him enough blood to be strong enough to fight against this.

Growling, I throw my feet forward and catch my fist in her back. She whirls around with canines out.

Quick scan of attacker: female, tall, eyes full of rage, and a pair of sharp nails dipped in blood.

I slam my fist into her stomach. She doubles over, gasping for breath. With a grunt, I launch a series of uppercuts into her jaw. One, two, three. Her teeth smack together as I knock her sideways. Hissing, she rears back and drags sharp nails down the side of my face, and pain shoots through my skin like jagged knives. I drop back and clench my fists before shooting another left hook into her stomach. She chokes and falls to her knees.

"Stop it." Blain's chilling voice freezes me to the spot. "Hit her again, and I'll shoot you."

I back off but stand firmly between her hunched figure and where Silas sprawls barely conscious on the floor. Victorious energy races through my bloodstream. Even though Blain stopped me, that was a fight I sure as hell won.

I swipe the blood off my face and fling it in the air where it splatters on her white suit. Slowly, she climbs to her feet.

"Nice going, Gwen," Kole finally speaks up in a strained voice. "You kicked her ass."

"Shut up." She hisses and smacks the glass of blood off the table. "You're not to speak."

My breath freezes in my throat. Her calm persona is obviously evaporating, and pushing her any harder might make her sanity snap in two. Once that happens, there's no telling how violent she may become, and I need to shift that focus from Kole and onto me.

"Just do whatever she says Kole," I say.

"It hasn't been so bad," he says, ignoring the both of us. "She's only made me show her the Blood Market hacking software."

"I said SHUT UP!" She screams the words into Kole's ears. I reach behind my back and slip my fingers around the gun. But when she wipes away the scowl, I loosen my grip on the steel. "Show me how to use the rest of the software."

Frowning, sweat drips down my forehead. If she's forcing Kole to show her how to use all the software, there's no way she's planning to let any of us live, even if Silas agrees to become her new second, which I could never let him do, least of all for me.

It's all down to Blain. He's the only one with a gun but me.

"Blain. You've never wanted to be a part of this world. There's no reason to do it now. I don't know how much she's giving you to do this, but I guarantee it's not worth it."

Blain just laughs. "You have no clue what you're in the middle of, Gwen. None of this was her idea. It was mine."

"What?" Frowning, I shake my head. How could any of this be his idea?

"I've always wanted to be a part of this world. It's in my blood. It's in my veins." He shifts the gun my way. "My family didn't want me to be one of them no matter what I did. So, I decided to make my own family. *My* way."

"Shut up, Blain." Isolde glares at him, and I have the sneaking suspicion the strange alliance they've created isn't so much an alliance at all.

"No." He glares back at her. "*I* came to *you*. The agreement was that I'd get Phantom off the streets in exchange for a place as your second-in-command. But you're breaking your word, asking *Silas* to join now."

Isolde lets out a tinkling laugh that sends a sharp shiver down my spine. "You didn't really think I'd keep you as my second, did you? You're one of them, the Nightshades."

"That was the deal." He narrows his eyes and shifts his focus on her. "You promised."

"And I dubbed you my second, as promised." She smiles and shakes her head. "*Acting* second. I was never going to keep you one step away from control, especially not after securing my spot as the most powerful vampire in this city. I know what you've been planning, Blain. You were going to kill me all along, just as soon as you had everything in its place.

"This is *my* vampire family, this is *my* plan, and *I* will be the one to gain control of this city." She stands tall and faces him with a cruel smile lining her thin lips.

The entire world falls to a standstill, and I don't dare breathe.

Blain swings the gun to where Isolde stands only inches from Kole, and my heart springs into action before my mind does.

"Kole, get down!" I scream.

A shot rings out and slams into Kole's shoulder. My heart sputters to a stop when he crumbles to the ground. I pull the Mad Hatter's gun from my waistband just as another shot rings out. It slices into Isolde's chest with a harsh wet slurp. She drops like an anchor, and her eyes roll back into her head. Blood pours from her wound and stains the floor a bright red, the color swirling into her bleached white hair.

With tears leaking from my eyes, I rush over to Kole's side and lift his head into my hands. "Are you okay? Kole, I'm sorry. I'm so, so sorry."

"One day, I hope things can be boring around here." He smiles, and I can't help but smile back.

"You're next." Blain's icy voice snatches my attention from Kole. He moves toward Silas with the gun aimed right at his face. "I've waited a long time for this. Orpheus, you bastard."

I turn. Silas has come to, his pale face highlighting the fact he has not had enough blood in days.

But he still stands. "What, did I hurt your pride when I beat the shit out of you that day?"

"You should have known it'd come back to bite you in the ass." Blain tightens his grip on the gun. "No one messes with me and gets away with it."

"Stop." I aim at Blain's back. "I have a gun."

Blain pauses, and Silas leans against the wall with one hand held tight to his wound. I hold the gun steady out in front of me and make my way toward Blain. My hands shake, but I ignore my nerves. If I've ever had to be strong, it's now.

"I told you to stay out of this, Gwen." He shakes his head. "But now I'm going to have to kill all of you, even though I didn't want to."

"Then don't do it, Blain." I slip around so he can see the gun in my hands. "Or I'll shoot you."

His finger slides against the trigger. "No, you won't."

That's the second time I've heard this today, and I swear to god, it'll be the last. "You better believe I will."

"Don't do it, Gwen," Silas breathes out, and that's all it takes to convince me which choice I need to make. I may never believe it's right to take a life, but at this moment, it isn't wrong either. If I stand here and do nothing, Silas will die.

Blain flinches toward Silas.

And I pull the trigger.

Only a soft *thump* punctuates the silence as the bullet soars out of the gun. It launches into Blain's skull, and he tumbles to the ground with a hole the size of a quarter in his forehead. A trail of blood leaks out of the wound and forms a puddle on the floor. Vacant eyes stare up at me. Hot tears burn my cheeks, and I turn away. I can't look at Blain's body. I don't want to see what I've done. Even though I had another choice, this was the only one I could bear to make. That doesn't mean it was right, but it doesn't mean it was wrong, either.

Silas groans as he slides to the floor. I rush over to his side and fall to my knees.

"Silas, are you okay?" I press light fingers against his head and examine the wound. Blood drips down his forehead and into his eyes. The gash is deep, but it's already beginning to heal.

"I'll live. But Gwen…"

"Don't say anything." I press a finger to his mouth. "He was about to shoot you."

Before he can argue, I lean down and brush my lips against his. Groaning, he reaches up and weaves his hand into my messy braid, pressing the softness of his lips deeply against my own.

The entire world falls away, though every nerve ending in my face sparks to life. He's my mate. And I wouldn't want it to be any other way.

CHAPTER 31
SILAS

A week passes, each day warmer than the next until winter's back begins to drift out of sight. The sun beams down on my deck, and I move two folding chairs outside while Tabby winds her way through my legs. She meows, and I reach down to ruffle her fur. Across the way, Mrs. Casey waves from her own deck while patting at her frizzing bush of hair. Just behind her, the power station chugs smog into the crisp air, reminding me this city is still steeped in dirt.

Some things never change, but some things definitely do.

Gwen Kane strides down the dock with a smile as bright as the sun. When she reaches me, she winds her arms around my neck and pulls me close, dropping a light kiss on my cheek. All the blood in my body rushes to that one spot. I sigh and press my nose into her coconut hair.

Gwen pulls back to hold up a box covered in wrapping paper, red and green with tiny cartoon balloons. "I got you something."

"You know it's not my birthday, right?" I take the box from her and pull at the paper.

"This is for all the ones I missed." She grins. "Don't worry, it's nothing big."

I rip away the paper, open the box, and peer down into its depths.

I can't help but smile. "You actually wrapped up my gun and brought it to me."

She pulls at her braid, the only way she's worn her hair since that night we fought my mother. "I thought it might come in handy one day."

"Thanks, Gwen." I chuckle and close the box before motioning us over to the folding chairs. I drop down, lean back my head, and let my face catch the sun. "I hope you're wrong, though. It's kind of nice having a quiet Towton City these days."

Gwen drops into the chair beside me. "You know it won't stay quiet for long."

"It never does."

"Kole says hi," Gwen says after several moments of easy silence.

"Is everything back to normal with you two?"

"Yeah. We both decided to forgive and forget." She frowns out at the river. "It's a little harder with Elliott, just because she can't even seem to forgive herself."

"My mother messed with her head," I say. "It can take some time to get over that."

"I just hope it doesn't take too long."

"And Phantom?"

Gwen sighs and settles her head against the back of the chair. She closes her eyes and lets the sun light her face. "It's good to have him back, but he's still as grumpy as ever. I think he feels a little embarassed that I had to save his ass."

"Well, I'm not embarassed that you saved *my* ass. In fact, it makes me fucking proud to be your mate."

She smiles, and it's the best thing I've ever seen in my life. "You better get used to it, too. Towton City still needs us, even if the gangs have gone quiet. They'll be back. The Saints haven't gone anywhere. And the humans still need our help. We've won for now, but it's not time to pack up our boots and weapons and everything else."

"So, what are you proposing, Gwen Kane?"

Her eyes flash when she meets my gaze. "I want to start our own House."

CHAPTER 32
GWEN
TWO WEEKS LATER

I smile at Mrs. Casey as she hobbles up to the table in front of me. A long line of humans and supernaturals stretch out behind her, all the way out the cathedral doors and down the street. Adjusting the crown on my head, I give her a nod.

"You know you didn't need to come here in person, Mrs. Casey," I say to her with a smile after glancing at Orpheus who sits beside me, wearing his own metallic crown. His amulet no longer dangles from his neck. He's let the world see him for who he really is.

She beams at us both. "Well. Now, you see, that's why I did come. You two deserve my recognition as the new King and Queen of the House of Roses and Rubies."

I can't help but grin at Orpheus. In the end, we did it, and here we are. Set up in the cathedral, leading our city into a better future. The House of Roses and Rubies is small, holding only Towton City within its boundaries, but there's always a chance we can extend our territory in the future. For now, this is enough.

It's more than enough.

The humans of the Coils have braved the streets. Some have moved to new buildings while others have started making the slums a safer place for those who want to stay. Elliott has been helping them. No one has been forced to give blood in weeks.

"Well, thank you, Mrs. Casey," Orpheus says. "You know you're more than welcome to join our House."

"I wouldn't join any other." She winks and drifts away while a tall fae with white hair and pale gray eyes strides up to us. I don't recognize him.

Alaric and Phantom both edge in closer. They decided to put aside their difference to act as guards for our new House. I was surprised the Saints agreed to it, but they were one of the first to pledge their loyalty to us. Seems taking out Isolde Thorn and Blain Shade earned me a lot of friends.

Orpheus leans forward with an arched brow. "Are you new to town?"

The fae just smiles, a wicked glint in his eye. "Name's Volker. I'm just passing through and wanted to check out the new House and its leaders. Everyone is talking about it."

I lift my chin, tension pounding in my skull. "I hope you don't plan to cause any trouble. We have no beef with any of the other Houses. We just want to protect our own."

"I can respect that," he says with a nod. "It's not easy what you've done. I wish you luck."

The fae wanders off without another word. I turn to Orpheus. "Think we need to worry about that? I can call Kole and have him do some research."

Kole and I are finally back on better terms, and he's taken up a role as the Head of Security. Not as a fighter himself but as a strategist. It means he can spend his time behind the computer, just how he wants it.

"No, I don't think so. But we do need to make sure we have added security set up around the city. Volker isn't here to cause trouble, but not everyone will feel the same. We've just staked claim on part of No Man's Land."

"Well, together I think we can take on anything." I lean in and kiss him. He slides his fingers into my hair, crushing my lips against his. Ever since I accepted our mating bond, I haven't been able to get enough of him, and I'm pretty sure the feeling is mutual.

"Ahem." Phantom clears his throat from behind us.

Orpheus just laughs.

Together, we turn to the next supernatural who approaches our table, set up to welcome everyone who wants to join our House. As it turns out, that's the entire city. The hours slowly tick by, and more and more humans and supernaturals drop in to pledge their loyalty.

And with every visit and every smile, the hope within me grows. Towton City might never be perfect, but with my mate by my side, our little slice of the world has a chance to be a better place for everyone.

It just took a lot of ass-kicking to get here.

Also by Jenna Wolfhart

The Mist King

Of Mist and Shadow

Of Ash and Embers

The Fallen Fae

Court of Ruins

Kingdom in Exile

Keeper of Storms

Tower of Thorns

Realm of Ashes

Prince of Shadows (A Novella)

Demons After Dark: Covenant

Devilish Deal

Infernal Games

Wicked Oath

Demons After Dark: Temptation

Sinful Touch

Darkest Fate

Hellish Night

ABOUT THE AUTHOR

Jenna Wolfhart spends her days tucked away in her writing studio in the countryside. When she's not writing, she loves to deadlift, rewatch Game of Thrones, and drink copious amounts of coffee.

Born and raised in America, Jenna now lives in England with her husband and her two dogs, Nero and Vesta.

www.jennawolfhart.com
jenna@jennawolfhart.com
tiktok.com/@jennawolfhart

www.ingramcontent.com/pod-product-compliance
Lightning Source LLC
Chambersburg PA
CBHW010448310726
48979CB00018B/2861/J

* 9 7 8 1 9 1 5 5 3 7 1 6 4 *